The Scoundrel Days
of Hobo Highbrow

The Scoundrel Days of Hobo Highbrow

Pål H. Christiansen

Translated by Jon Buscall

fabula

First Published by Tiden Norsk Forlag 2002
Norwegian title: Drømmer om storhet
© Pål H Christiansen 2008
ISBN 978-82-90812-09-1
Printed and bound by AIT Trykk Otta AS, Norway 2008
Cover illustration: Arve Rød
Typesetting: Gazoline AS, 2008

Forlaget Fabula
P.O.Box 97
N-1321 Stabekk
Norway

www.forlaget-fabula.no

"*I am nothing.*
I shall always be nothing.
I can only want to be nothing.
Apart from this, I have in me all the dreams in the world."

ÁLVARO DE CAMPOS

Some men make a big deal of the fact that women need a bit of extra time getting ready in the morning. They work themselves up into an enormous rage shouting abuse and obscenities at the wall, the furniture and fittings. But is there any use in kicking the living daylights out the bathroom door or threatening to go on ahead in the hope of cutting down the time you spend waiting? Doesn't it just make things worse and the time spent waiting even more difficult to bear? No, it's probably better to sit down and wait until she's ready – no matter how long it takes. Along with writing grammatically correct Norwegian, this is one of the most important things I have learnt in life.

I was in Helle's kitchen, listening to the sound of the taps running in the bathroom. I'd bet money that she was just at the point of shampooing her hair. She was no doubt kneading the rejuvenating liquid deep down into the roots. After that it would be rinsed, balsam applied and then the rest of her body would be treated to the same intense cleansing procedure.

The clock on the wall said eight-thirty. Helle was in the midst of a very hectic period, getting on with things. She planned to redecorate the kitchen. The fridge had been moved to the middle of the floor together with the spice rack, notice board and a reproduction of a painting by Gauguin depicting a woman with a child in her arms. The plan, as I understood it, was to paint the walls green and the kitchen units were to be restored to their original redish colour.

There is one thing I've learnt about women, I thought. They con themselves into thinking that life will be better after re-decorating. That life will once again be full of possibilities. But the fact of the matter is that it is hard work alone that gets you to the gates of heaven.

I went into the living-room and stood in front of the book-shelf. The balcony door was wide open and the sounds of the city floated up from the street. Kids were shouting to each other on their way to school, and I could hear the sound of the passing tram and the trundling din of the refuse truck mov-ing from building to building.

I could say a lot of good things about Helle, but when it came to the organisation of her bookcase, well, she left a lot to be desired. Right in front of me, for example, was a copy of a certain Howard Humpelfinger's *Erogenous Zones in the Middle Ages*. Humpelfinger's publishers would have done hu-manity a massive favour if they had recalled every edition and pulped them. The text was, alas, so full of typos it was practically unreadable. But what was worse was that Helle had managed to put *Erogenous Zones* next to the Norwegian dic-tionary for crying out loud! These books are diametrically op-posed to one another: they are like chalk and cheese.

The Norwegian dictionary is a splendidly useful tool. You get an answer to every question you could possibly imagine about the Norwegian language with a precision and turn of phrase that's almost worth dying for. The edition on Helle's shelf that I picked up was from 1982 but that didn't matter. I don't really think there's any harm in going back to the earlier documentation on the language. The orthography of 1917 has its positive sides and there's a lot of good things to say about the version from 1907, but I don't dare go back any earlier.

I sat for quite a long time on the sofa, lost in the definitions and explanations contained in this wondrous tome on the Norwegian language, whilst Helle showered on and on as if there were no tomorrow. I've always had a liking for the kind of word that precisely and ingeniously describes a particular phenomena, being or object in Norwegian like, say, "GRÅTASS". A "gråtass" is a grey, wolf-like animal that pads or shuffles about. Sitting on the sofa, flicking through the dictionary, I could imagine that wolf-like creature in the border country between Norway and Sweden, hungry and alone, hunting for a sheep to sink its teeth into.

I heard the shower turn off and there was a moment's silence. What now? Was she covering herself with that delicious cream I liked to sniff whenever I went into her bathroom? Or perhaps it was time to clean her teeth next? I stood up and walked a few steps towards the bathroom.

The door opened. Helle came out with a towel wrapped around her midriff, her hair wet. She looked shamelessly cheerful and happy as she walked across the living-room floor, apparently not noticing me as I stood there with the Norwegian dictionary in my hand, a sleepy expression on my face. We had gone late to bed the previous evening after a game of Scrabble which had led to several interesting discussions about the correct spelling of words like PSORIASIS, CANTANKEROUS, and ANTIDISESTABLISHMENTARIANISM. When it came to language, Helle was one of the few people I trusted on the planet, and one I could really test myself against.

After I had won the game with the help of the word YAJNAS, we had rounded off the evening with a Lumumba, each with plenty of rum, before going to bed. As we lay there falling into deep sleep we were like two children without a care in the world.

11

"There IS such a word as YAJNAS actually," I said. "It says so here."

"Where?" said Helle.

"In the dictionary. A Yajna, also called 'yagna', is a ritual sacrifice with a specific objective."

"Okay," said Helle.

She let go of the bath towel. At that very same moment a breeze blew the curtains so they looked like a flag over the living-room floor. And with the wind, a gust of intense feelings blew right through me: Helle was standing there laughing, naked. I stared at her breasts. They heaved up and down as if eager to venture out and conquer new places. I walked towards her, wrapping her in my arms, not caring in the slightest if I got wet or soaked my white shirt. This was the woman I loved.

Helle's apartment was on the fourth floor. Whilst she went and got dressed I went out on to the balcony to enjoy the view. The dustbin men had parked just outside Helle's building and an orange-clad man was wheeling a bin which he loaded and emptied into the back of the cart. There was something familiar about him, I thought, leaning over, but he wandered out of sight. It's not a great job being a dustbin man. But it keeps you fit and you're finished early each day. A superb job for a poet, I thought.

It was September 1st and the whole of eastern Norway was caught up in a heat wave. It didn't really suit me because I was waiting for autumn. Besides, I had recently started working on the only manuscript I had any real belief in. I sensed that if I could just get it together I would finally make it as a writer. The only thing I had to do was improve the text so it would make more than a fleeting impression on the nation's critics. I was looking forward to getting down to writing my novel. I planned to do this during the autumn as the nights drew in and the cold forced you to remain inside except when absolutely necessary.

Autumn was without a doubt *my* season. It was a time for reflection. A time to consider the true meaning of life. It was the time to carry on building my masterpiece, taking up where I had left off in the spring, distracted by all the birdsong and light that came with the season. When hadn't I written my best work, if it wasn't the autumn? Under the dim light of my old desk lamp, wearing my smoking jacket, my words had wings that soared above the rain that fell upon the dark concrete city outside my window.

The tram was just leaving as we left the apartment building and came out onto street level. This was reason enough to follow Helle to work, and then continue on foot through Slottsparken and down to the paper's offices. Helle was wearing the flowery summer dress I liked so much and she had put her hair up which made her look more like a teacher.

"What are you teaching today?" I said smiling, taking her hand in mine.

"Iambic pentameter and trochaics," said Helle.

"Interesting," I said, happy that teenagers today still learned classical verse forms.

"Well, I suppose that depends on the audience," said Helle.

"What about anapest?" I wondered.

"We'll get to that later," said Helle.

"You can spend a whole lifetime on iambic pentameter alone," I said.

Helle straightened my tie when we reached the entrance of the school. Then she kissed me and walked off through the school playground. Helle was a popular teacher and a lot of pupils said "Hi" as she went. A couple of boys even fought to hold the door open for her but they ended up falling over each other in their struggle. I watched as Helle opened the door herself and finally disappeared from view.

After the previous evening's Scrabble-contest I felt like a word master, so I sat right down at my desk as soon as I got to the paper. Four or five pieces were already finished and I started work on an article about Oslo's nightlife, penned by an experienced journalist who was wellknown for boasting that he never made a mistake.

Everyone makes a mistake – from time to time! It's inhuman to not make a single tiny mistake. You forget a letter, a conjunction, or an apostrophe because you're writing so quickly, so IT'S becomes ITS or CAN'T becomes CANT. These are the kind of everyday errors a busy journalist makes and there is no reason to be embarrassed about them. "We learn from our mistakes," Holm, the paper's editor, liked to remind us whenever we had a training seminar. But if you didn't learn from your mistakes, you wouldn't amount to very much.

As I carefully read the article, I discovered a mistake. Two words had drifted apart. Instead of CANNOT it said CAN NOT. This wasn't a linguistic mistake, as such. It was more of a hesitation that had got in the way; a erroneous tap of the spacebar that took only a tenth of a second.

The next article was about a-ha, who were going to cobble their talents together in an attempt to get the band on the right track again after each member of the band had been occupied with their individual projects for a number of years. Morten Harket with his solo work, Magne Furuholmen with his art work and film music, and Pål Waaktaar with the band he had started with his wife, Savoy.

This was great news both for myself and the world in general. I often listened to a-ha's sophisticated, melancholic pop music whilst writing. Indeed, I'd often been inspired to push myself that little bit further whenever I thought of Morten, Magne and Pål. a-ha were one of my favourite groups and a positive force in Norwegian and international culture. That they were still up for it now, in spite of everything, the hard work, the dwindling record sales, was good news that deserved column-space in the paper.

The article didn't delve into who had done what or who had argued with who during the preceding years. But it was no secret that Morten Harket and Pål Waaktaar's relationship had been strained for a while now. They were two strong personalities who could clash head to head with each other, no doubt about it. Still, it was really good to hear that they were getting on again, but even better news that a new album was in the works.

The journalist had written the band's name practically every other time without a hyphen. I corrected this error and sent the article back to the news desk and decided to listen to my a-ha records at the first opportunity.

At lunchtime I went to the canteen to get some food. Holm, the editor-in-chief, was sitting at a window table talking to a couple of journalists from the features-desk. It surprised me because ordinarily he would have ditched everything in this kind of weather and headed off for the golf course.

I walked past the counter a couple of times before I managed to make up my mind about what to have for lunch. A lot of it looked very tempting, but I wasn't the kind of man to be enticed by healthy-looking lettuce leaves so I made do with half a cheese roll and a cup of coffee then left again.

Holm and the other two who were with him glanced across at me as I left the canteen. It gave me the feeling that they were talking about me. I momentarily contemplated returning to join them at their table to discuss the Hubbing-case, but quickly dismissed the idea and returned to my desk instead. Once there I sat enjoying my lunch on my own, trying to remember the title of a poem by Olaf Bull. The first verse went something like:

> Midsummer is already sliding towards fall,
> And the tree tops stoop under the burden –
> Oh, the autumn emits a distant call,
> Before a single bough is golden!

I thought the poem was in Bull's collection *Stjernerne* (The Stars) from 1924 but I wasn't sure. It might also be from *Nye Digte* (New Poems) which came out in 1913, where "In the snow" is also to be found amongst them. In the end I called Helle on her mobile phone but she didn't answer. I left a message on her voice-mail, hoping she would call me back as soon as she was free.

I remained seated, finishing my lunch, and my thoughts turned to my novel. The opening was quite good and struck the right kind of tone: the protagonist returns from a long journey across the desert and discovers that something isn't quite right. All the birds have disappeared. It is silent in his garden; there's not even a sparrow cheeping away. He climbs up a tree hoping to find out what's going on but there's not a bird in sight. Not in his garden or any of his neighbours' gardens. He remains sitting there up in the tree for the entire day, only climbing down when evening comes, having decided to dedicate his life to persuading the birds to return.

The next piece to be checked was the editorial. It was written by Holm and took up the Hubbing-case. In it Holm questioned national security and the role of the media. The fact that he had completed the editorial so early in the day meant that he was in a hurry to get out of the office. This was also, no doubt, why there were a number of typos: NAITIONAL. MEEDIA. There was also at least one missing preposition. If it was a hole-in-one he was after, this particular piece of work was well over par. I didn't have a chance to reflect upon the article's content, otherwise I would have been sitting there for the rest of the day.

Helle rang just after lunch.

" 'Sommerens Forlis'," she said. "It's in *Nye Digte*."

"Damn," I said. "I was certain it was in *Stjernerne*."

"Are you sure you're not mixing it up with 'In the Autumn'?" Helle wondered.

"Possibly," I said. "But at least I remembered how the first verse went."

"It's a very sad poem," said Helle.

The heat hit me as I left the office, walking towards Karl Johan. The day's duties were all taken care of so I could now start thinking about my own writing with a clear conscience.

My previous literary endeavors were little more than the first phase of a dawning career as a writer. *The Letter*, from 1984, was about someone who needed to leave to create his own kind of space. In that space, anything could happen! In *Harry Wasn't All There*, a collection of short stories, I explored the form of the short story for the one and only time in my life. In *Berry Picking* (from 1990), a collection of poems, I utilised the sonnet form.

Things had been quiet for a while. They really had. I hadn't published anything for more than ten years. Sure, I'd written and written but I hadn't got anywhere. A new spirit and era had swept me out of favour with editors at publishing houses where once I had been warmly welcomed. First I stood out in the corridor, cap in hand, waiting for another chance, whilst the powers of the new age swept past me in the queue. Later, I didn't even make it to the corridor. I wandered, lost in a literary wintery wilderness, year after year after year.

Was I bitter? No. Had I given up on this country's lack of cultural prowess? Yes! What did the average Norwegian know about what it cost in terms of effort and what you had to deny yourself to dare to take your dreams seriously? What did they know about the road to success?

a-ha knew it. They had felt the hunger like young figures from a Knut Hamsun novel stranded in London. They'd searched high and low for food amongst the rubbish and scraps of the city. They lived in hope and in the certainty that they had something that was just too big for Little Old Norway. It was like a force that exploded inside them, driving them far, far away from social-democratic Norwegian self-righteousness. Sure, they had problems. Difficulties lay in their way. But they tackled them one by one! Some people say that it was just luck. But I just want to tell those doubters that it had nothing to do with luck. It was to do with talent and how Harket, Furuholmen and Waaktaar were put together.

I turned onto Karl Johan and carried on in the direction of Slottet – the palace. People were making the most of the good weather, sitting at tables outside restaurants wearing sunglasses and drinking beer. I stopped outside Tanum, the bookstore, looking in at the window-display. All the latest detective novels were there crammed in next to the cookbooks by celebrity cooks and other people who claimed they knew something about cooking. There was no serious literary fiction in sight, although the Norwegian Dictionary had been given its own little corner, no doubt on account of the fact that it was the start of the new school year. With a shake of my head, I carried on.

I had never doubted that I had something more than all those middle-of-the-road writers who tried and actually managed to get their work published. Those writers had nothing of any great consequence to say really, because here in Norway a writer is expected to publish a novel or two every year. So they write and it gets published and bought by all the public libraries and that's the icing on the cake for these mindless so-called artists.

To be honest, I mustn't make out that I was bigger than I really was at that moment! Everything I'd written up to this point was like the work of a journeyman compared to that which I was now going to write. But now the bells were ringing! Even I had to admit that the Nordic Council's Literary Award was well within my grasp. And the need to sit down and write grew deeper and deeper within me as I walked along the streets of Oslo. I was like a loaf of bread that had risen and was about to spill out over the baking tin, out of the oven and conquer the world!

What was it Rainer Maria Rilke once said? Being an artist means not numbering and counting, but ripening like a tree, which doesn't force its sap, and stands confidently in the storms of spring, not afraid that summer may not come afterwards. It does come. But it comes only to those who are patient, who are there as if eternity lay before them, unconcerned, silent and vast.

I have to admit that my patience had been tried now and then. But now it was finally autumn – my time of the year.

I crossed Universitetsgaten and then Karl Johan and walked towards the statues of two of the greatest Norwegian writers, Ibsen and Bjørnson, standing each on their pedestal in front of the National Theatre. The two of them were perhaps tempted to give a self-satisfied smile to themselves but they undoubtedly had more experience under their belt than 99% of the people who called themselves writers. I stopped to look at their faces: Bjørnson slightly pompous, Ibsen deadly serious. They were two giants, each on their own little mound. Two artists who had left their mark on this country, each in their own special way.

But what about Wergeland, I wondered? What had happened to him?

I glanced around, finally spotting him all alone on the other side of the street. So that's where they had put him! I supposed it was only apt that he had a more prominent position in relation to parliament, given his status.

Wergeland, though, seemed satisfied to be on his own when I crossed the street to look at him. And compared to the other two gentlemen, I decided there was something more life-like and coarse about Wergeland.

I glanced up and saw the tram approaching from Stortingsgaten. I crossed the street again and ran over towards the tram stop. The bus to Tårnåsen was coming from the opposite direction just as I rounded the corner.

I was determined to go back to my flat and get on with my writing as soon as I got off the tram. On the way, however, I stopped to glance in through the window of the Four Hens. There wasn't anyone I knew inside, just a couple of old codgers, each nursing a beer.

I had recently read the proofs for an article about how important it is to drink sufficient liquid in hot weather. Otherwise things can get pretty nasty for the intricate mechanism universally known as the body. The article recommended that you consume 10-15 litres of liquid a day, but I took this with a pinch of salt. Nevertheless, I hesitated, feeling my shirt sticking to my back. My head was heavy but my arms were surprisingly light. It occurred to me that my inspiration might vanish if I didn't do something about the precarious situation immediately.

Hjort was behind the bar as usual, washing up glasses whilst humming along to the big hit of the summer by Hubert and the Hamsters, "Kick My Behind".

"Don't say a word," he said. "You want a pint of beer!"

"No head on it," I said.

"Are you sure you wouldn't rather try the new beer from Monrovia?" asked Hjort.

"Where?"

"They brew good beer there," said Hjort.

I had no idea how much Hjort got for promoting some old shit from Liberia, but I did know that I was going to have a pint with no head on it. Thankfully he soon ceased hounding me to try the Monrovian beer and began filling a glass, whilst I watched carefully, making sure everything was as it should be.

"Too much froth," I said.

"Wait a minute," said Hjort.

"I'm not paying for froth," I said.

Hjort got rid of the froth and carried on filling the glass. He then shoved the glass across the bar counter. I took a sip, savouring the moment as the beer began to restore balance to my body.

"Have you noticed that Higgins smells like rubbish these days?" asked Hjort.

"No," I replied.

"He was in here yesterday and I had to ask him to leave," said Hjort. "Go home and take a shower," I told him.

"Hmm," I said,

"I'm running a business here," said Hjort.

"Higgins is an artist," I said.

"That's as old as the hills," said Hjort.

Was it really? Was it too much to expect that artists washed themselves as often as the rest of us? I didn't think so, but I was open to other opinions. It was a free country, after all. But there were limits, naturally. Still, something had to be said if it was really affecting others. The trouble was that I now wondered if that moment had come.

"What do you mean by smells?" I asked.

"Exactly what I said," said Hjort.

"Did you really mean *stinks*?"

"I mean that he smells," said Hjort.

Helle entered the bar carrying a bag from COLOUR WORLD. I immediately had a sinking feeling. If she thought she was going to take me back to her place to paint her kitchen, she had another thing coming. I had more important things to do, and told her so – in a nice way, of course.

"I thought I'd find you here," she said.

"Really?" I said. "You two think a lot of strange things. Hjort claims he knew I came here to have a pint."

"Pure guess work," said Hjort.

"I'm actually on my way home to WRITE," I said. "I've got a novel to write, and if I don't do it who do you think is going to do it?"

"I want to go out to Huk," said Helle.

"To Huk?" I said as congenially as possible, then leaned forward and kissed her on the brow. I put my arms around her and pulled her into me. She smelt wonderfully fresh, with just a faint fragrance of green soap and old sandwiches, suggesting that she had come straight from work.

"We can have a barbecue on the beach," said Helle.

I looked in her carrier bag. She'd bought paint, sandpaper, putty filler and white spirit. And there right at the bottom were a couple of utensils of dubious origin.

"I bought a litre and half for starters," she said.

"Sensible," I said, looking through the bag.

"They wanted to sell me 10 litres but I said no," Helle explained.

"Good girl!" I said.

I finally managed to get hold of the utensils and took them out for closer inspection. There was something with a plastic handle and straggly bristles.

"What on earth is this?" I said.

"A brush," said Helle.

"You've got a couple of crap brushes there then," I said. "Don't you know that cheap brushes moult faster than a bitch in season?"

"They'll be fine," said Helle.

"No, they won't," I said. "You clearly don't know what you're talking about. Hjort will back me up on this, won't you?"

But Hjort had gone and hidden in the kitchen somewhere, so I had no support on hand.

"There are two things that are important in life," I said. "The first is to make sure you drink plenty of water. The other is to use quality brushes when you paint."

Someone had been in the apartment. I could smell it. A strange mixture of sweat, mouthwash and something even worse. Was it perhaps my own bodily decay that had finally kicked in with a vengeance? I had been expecting this since I turned forty.

The mess in my apartment was worse than usual. Boxes of books stood everywhere and there were bedclothes in a pile on the floor. It looked like someone was moving in and moving out at the same time. As for the sofa, well it seemed to have disappeared completely.

I looked everywhere without success, falling over the boxes of books. Several hundred copies of *The Letter* lined the walls whilst *Harry Wasn't All There* was in front of the bed. *Berry Picking* lay in a solitary box under the kitchen table. The boxes of books had their uses but also disadvantages. In the kitchen, I put hot things on them and in the bathroom I put my feet up on them when the floor was wet.

When guests visited the apartment I employed the boxes as makeshift stools.

"There's nothing like putting your arse down on a pile of poetry," Higgins liked to say just before farting. It was his way of giving highfaluting poetry a taste of grim reality.

I sat down at my desk and collected my thoughts together, thinking about writing. The first step in such a complex ritual of creative writing was to put on my smoking jacket. Trouble was I hadn't seen it for weeks. Step two: well, that was thinking things through which I usually did on the sofa. Dammit! Losing the sofa was like a kick in the teeth.

To explain: My new novel was about a person who achieves his dream of building the most perfect birdhouse anyone has ever seen. He spends years of his life learning carpentry. After that he makes one birdhouse after another, placing each in the forest. The protagonist's ultimate goal is to tempt the birds back. Does he succeed? Or doesn't he? It was too soon to say.

I wondered if I shouldn't perhaps already know the ending. Should I know my protagonist so well that I knew where it would take him if he realised his dreams in full?

The answer was a resounding: No! There was no point in a novelist writing a story if he knew the ending already. That was my opinion at least and I was sticking to it.

So far so good. Now the time was ripe to transport myself into a suitable atmosphere for creative writing so I commenced stage three of my ritual by going over to the bookshelf to find *Hunting High and Low*. I was in the habit of listening to Morten Harket sing "Take on Me" as an upbeat preamble to an animated and inspired writing session. That man had a God-given talent, that was sure. And when he turns on that falsetto of his in "Take On Me" the only thing to be done is to forget all those meaningless earthly things like TIDYING UP and DOING THE LAUNDRY and WRITING POSTCARDS to old acquaintances. No, the only thing to do is to scribble down creative musings until your pencil snaps and your body says 'Thank you'.

I stood still in front of the bookcase. Something had happened since I was here last. My old record player had been replaced by a spanking new CD-player with massive speakers and buttons all over the place. What's more, my old vinyl records were nowhere to be seen.

It wasn't the first time I had been faced with adversity. Actually, I was quite used to it. If adversity ennobles, then I figured I was at least a Count by now, sitting down at my desk again, gripping my last straw – my pencil sharpener.

Sharpening pencils has saved many a writer from embarrassment. Take a Hemingway, for example; a certain Ernest Miller Hemingway. Born 1899 in Oak Park, Illinois, USA, Hemingway needed to have a certain number of sharpened pencils laid out in front of him before he started writing each morning. He would have anything between five and seventy pencils lined up, depending on his mood. During a short period when he lived in Key West in Florida he sharpened 133 pencils every morning. After a while, as his finances improved, he had people to take care of this for him which was surely much better than during his young days when he struggled as an unknown writer in Paris.

Another strange thing about Hemingway, as I recall, was that he STOOD UP when writing. How he came up with something as silly as this, I have no idea, but if it worked, it worked. I was not the kind of writer to get mixed up in how my colleagues set about their business.

I looked over at the bed. Given that the sofa was missing, I decided I could lie on the bed as a temporary solution. It usually worked as well as Hemingway's routine of standing up. So I moved over to the bed and lay down, getting comfy under the duvet.

The telephone rang before I had even made a start.

"What are doing?" said Haagen.

"Right now, I am doing bed, " I said. "If that's a phrase you're okay with."

"You're asleep?"

"Call it what you will, but I call it writing."

"Ah, I get it. You making any progress?" wondered Haagen.

Was it the novel he was talking about? Or was it my new year's resolution to get rid of a couple of linguistic habits I had stuck with since childhood, and primarily when speaking? I had always insisted on using: "To whom am I speaking?" instead of the more common "Who am I speaking to?"

"You haven't seen my a-ha records, have you?" I said.

"Have you looked under the sofa?" said Haagen, rather vaguely. But at least he had a suggestion.

I looked over to where the sofa had once stood. There on the floor were a couple of odd socks covered in dust, as well as something that looked like a crispbread with goat's cheese. Or maybe it was liver pâté? I hadn't had anything like that in the apartment for as long as I could remember, and I had no intention of investigating the matter at that particular point.

"Nope," I said.

"Have you ever heard Hubert and the Hamsters?" asked Haagen. "They've really hit upon something."

"I'll stick to a-ha, thank you very much," I said.

"I have to run," said Haagen. "I'm playing Ulf Lundell's "Öppna landskap" in three minutes.

"Good luck!"

"See you later at Huk," said Haagen.

How on earth had Haagen got wind of the idea that someone had suggested going to Huk? Or to put it another way, IF I was going to Huk, it would have been for a romantic encounter with Helle and not for a night out with the lads.

Now I knew full well that this city is full of gossip and rumours. I'd personally experienced this several times. If, for example, I got the hiccups in Akersgata, I could be sure that

Haagen or Higgins had heard about it within an hour.

I closed my eyes, shutting the world out for a moment. I let my mind wander into daydreams and envisioned the moment when my creative prowess would really kick in. I would be like a power station – able to light up an entire city. A flickering head amongst a storm of self-confidence, green waves and a smile from ear to ear.

Right in the middle of this I would stand with my feet firmly on the ground, my head half way to heaven. My words would bellow like claps of thunder amidst a raging storm or flutter softly like butterfly kisses on an innocent cheek.

And the audience?

Young and old would lay at my feet, hanging on my every word as I travelled from town to town, from sold-out gig to gig, reading to women as quiet as mice in the nation's public libraries.

The delivery bicycle from Herman's stood leaning against the wall outside the shop, looking rather dejected. The handle-bars were crooked and the basket on the front had a dent in it. Even the hand-painted sign under the crossbar had seen better days: it now read 'Herman's Corn' instead of 'Herman's Corner' as it should have.

The shop was chilly and I moved slowly between the shelves. Ordinarily I was a considerable consumer of 15 watt light-bulbs and crab sold by the kilo. But now I was out shopping for something for dinner. I was dead hungry and wanted pasta with tomato sauce quicker than you could say Jack Robinson. As soon as I'd eaten, I'd get on with crafting literature again.

"Your groceries are over here," said Herman from behind the counter.

"Are they?" I said, notably surprised.

"Give my regards to your wife and tell her we didn't have any mineral water," said Herman.

"My wife?" I said.

"I forgot to mention it on the phone," said Herman.

Oh, how familiar we'd become! I thought. And how had he got the idea I was married? It was more than I knew, and I had no intention of discussing the matter further with him either. All I wanted was Dolmio. Now.

"You looking for some Dolmio?" said Herman.

31

"Yes," I said.

"It's on order. We should have some next week," said Herman.

I felt irritation tingle throughout my body. So, it was the old game again. "It's on order." "We'll have some in tomorrow." "Next week." At least he was honest enough not to try and bullshit me. Otherwise he might as well pack his goods together and leave for the Store Owners Retirement Home in Lanzarote.

"You're going out to Huk to barbecue in this lovely weather, I understand," said Herman, lifting up a carrier bag from behind the counter and putting it on the conveyor.

"Someone seems to think so," I said.

"That'll be 233 kroner," said Herman.

I looked inside the bag. There were all kinds of different sausages, beer, fizzy drinks, and a disposable grill which included a very practical disposable bin-bag. It was a typical carrier bag for a picnic. A typical Huk-bag.

"Say 'hello' to your wife and say that I didn't have the mineral water she wanted," said Herman.

"Didn't you just tell me that?" I wondered.

"Sorry," said Herman, blushing.

I looked closer at him. If the truth be told he fancied Helle, the dirty old git!

"Do you want any cash back?" asked Herman.

I ignored the question and made my way out of the shop. Herman followed me out, nodding and pointing to the bike.

"The lad really messed up big time today," he said.

Two quick toots of a car horn got me up and out of my chair and over to the window. I caught sight of a blue refuse truck through the entrance of the backyard, and just after that there

32

was a ring at the door.

"Can you bring a towel for Haagen?" said Helle in the intercom.

"Why?" I wanted to know.

"Hurry up," said Helle, ignoring my question.

I sat down again at my desk and glanced at my notes. What had I written in the last couple of minutes? My handwriting was getting worse with age. I had to snap out of it or I would end up dyslectic.

I sat there for a moment listening and then wondered if I really should go out. Maybe I should just pretend that nothing had happened and carry on writing, especially as I had managed to get going without the sofa, my smoking jacket, or my a-ha records spinning on my old record player.

The doorbell rang again. I've got my lovely notebook, I thought. I'd got that as a Christmas present from Holm, my editor, at the paper. It was covered in PVC with Verdens Gang written in glittering gold lettering and a tiny padlock. If I took it with me I might be able to manage a couple of scenes in between sausages.

Helle was sitting in the truck, talking to Higgins when I came out. It sounded like they were in the middle of a serious discussion about the highs and lows of sandwiches, and in particular whether or not to wrap sandwiches in baking paper. I got in and let them continue their conversation as we drove towards Bygdøy.

"If 800 pupils use half a meter of tin foil every day five days a week. How much is that?" asked Higgins.

"Exactly two kilometres," said Helle. "But you're forgetting a couple of really important things."

"Like what?" said Higgins.

"To start with most pupils have a plastic sandwich box,"

said Helle. "Some of them use a bit of baking paper between their sandwiches, but all the same."

"What about the others?" said Higgins.

"A lot of kids don't even take a packed lunch to school at all," said Helle. "They buy Cola and a bun or muffin from 7-Eleven."

"Just a minute!" I said, interrupting them. "Can I ask something?"

"Go on then," said Helle.

"Have you brought the Scrabble board?" I wanted to know.

"It's in here," Helle said, patting her bag.

Higgins had given up on the baking paper and was ready to talk cars. As a hard working sculptor he had long complained about his lack of wheels. And given that he made art out of the rubbish and leftovers of contemporary buy-and-throw-away culture, he'd previously noted that a refuse truck wouldn't be a bad investment. Now, in possession of one, he had the right vehicle to achieve his dreams.

"What do you think?" he said, glancing over at me as we ground to a halt in the rush hour traffic along Bygdøy Allé.

"Great!" I said, enthusiastically. "Nice seats, nice lines and plenty of room."

I certainly wasn't going to be the one to stifle aspiring Norwegian artists with negative vibes. The only negative thing was the smell. I sensed the weak odour of rubbish wafting towards me from the driving seat. It sounded as if Hjort's sensitive nose had picked up something that had missed the rest of us.

"Does it drink a lot of petrol?" I said.

"What do you mean?" said Higgins, immediately on the defensive.

"He wants to know how many kilometres it does to the

litre?" said Helle.

"Are you kidding me or what?" said Higgins. "It uses diesel!"

Helle's mobile telephone rang. Haagen was on the outskirts of Frogner Park and wanted a lift. Higgins turned the vehicle out of the queue and down a side street.

We eventually located him on Halvdan Svartes gate. He was waiting by the statue of Christian Krogh. What those two would have to say to each other wasn't worth talking about. Krogh sat there on his massive sculpted behind, looking inspired whilst Haagen stood there sweating his socks off, dressed in a dark suit, a saxophone under his arm. He must have played "Öppna landskap" at record speed and run like the wind to get there.

We weren't the only ones with the idea of going to the beach. A steady stream of cars and people were heading out towards Bygdøy. It was as if every single last drop of warmth had to be squeezed out of the sun before everyone settled for wrapping up in long overcoats to fend off the biting autumn wind.

There were those, of course, that went south during the autumn and winter to escape the cold. Writers and other lucky souls in receipt of a government stipend, able to travel as much as they wanted, eking out their pennies in warmer, cheaper countries. I could see them there, trying to be creative amidst a red wine-induced haze which lasted from the moment they got up in the morning to the time they went to bed.

I didn't envy them a single penny of their grants, even though I had never received anything other than the Professor Hybel Stipend. I'd received three-thousand kroner for that, which just about covered a dentist's bill and the purchase of a pencil sharpener.

After the usual discussion about where we were going to sit down, Haagen settled the subject good and proper by wandering off with the food. We followed as best we could and when we caught up we found him on his knees on the sand in the process of trying to light the disposable BBQ.

Once the BBQ was ready, Higgins took over. He laid out several different kinds of sausage in an intricate pattern pointing inwards, obviously designed to maximise the space on the grill to the full. I noted that there were grill sausages and wieners as well as something shorter that I didn't quite recognise. What where they? Spanish sausages from Santiago de Compostela, perhaps, with chilli and good luck wishes? No, it was probably just a couple of squashed wieners. Mind you it was very confusing that they sold different sized sausages all squashed together in the same packet. I had to talk to Herman about this, as soon as I got the opportunity.

"Grill or wiener?" asked Higgins when they were finally ready.

"I beg your pardon?" I said.

"Grill or wiener sausage?" repeated Higgins.

"Don't you know that we writers no longer engage in public debate?" I said.

Higgins shrugged his shoulders.

"It was Bull and those boys who did that sort of thing," I said. "Bjørnson and Wergeland too. And Welhaven."

"We're talking about having something to eat, Hobo," said Higgins.

"Forget about Bull," I said. "He's not important."

"Why?" said Helle.

"He was just a bit of a lush, very partial to the bottle," I said.

"Just?" said Helle.

"Well, perhaps not just," I said. "But don't tell me that he didn't like his grog."

Higgins lifted up the tongs in a threatening way, so I eased off a little, noticing simultaneously that it was as if Helle and Haagen had moved a little closer to one another. They looked at me with the threatening glare of the mob.

"Yes?" I inquired.

"Grill or wiener?" asked Higgins.

"This is going to be bloody difficult," I said.

After we'd eaten it was time for Scrabble. It was easier said than done because the ground was full of roots and clumps of grass that made it difficult to lay the board flat. No matter where I put it, it remained at sixes and sevens.

"Damn," I said, as the letters slid off the board, falling down into pine needles and rubbish.

"What's the matter?" said Helle.

"Just a load of crap," I said, irritated, sweat now forming on my brow.

"Calm down," said Hele.

"It's all over the place here," I said. "It's a bloody mess."

"Don't worry, I'll sort it out," said Helle.

"It's like building an airport on a cliff," I said.

Helle took her jumper out of her shoulder bag and in one effortless movement lay it flat on the ground, with one sleeve supporting the Scrabble board from underneath. I gently kissed her on the forehead. Her practical good sense was such an endearing quality and I loved her for it.

Haagen and Higgins discussed organizing a get-together at the Four Hens. Haagen had an idea that Higgins' truck could be of use although I didn't quite understand how. I had half an ear on what they were saying whilst waiting for Helle.

"A touring gallery?" said Higgins.

"Not quite," said Haagen.

"A touring orchestra?" asked Higgins.

"No, not quite that either," said Haagen.

No, it wasn't always quite that easy, I figured. If you only had to think of yourself there wasn't that much to worry about. I looked at Helle. A gentle breeze wafted through her hair, and she looked to have her thoughts on something other than me or the game of Scrabble. What was she thinking about? School essays that still had to be corrected? The kitchen that needed to be painted? Iambs and trochees? There was plenty to think about in her everyday life just as in mine.

"Can you hurry up?" I said.

"Are we in a rush?" asked Helle.

"It's all about keeping the tempo up," I said. "About not losing your concentration."

"That's the difference between men and women," said Helle.

"Really?" I said, spotting the beginnings of an interesting conversation.

"As a woman I see Scrabble as a continuous, never-ending process," said Helle. "It's all about the joy of words, the exploration of the language. That's the main point of it."

"And what about men?" I said.

"You're just obsessed with winning," Helle said.

Of course she was talking rubbish, but she was so quick and articulate that I had to concede – just for a moment, mind. I was very proud of her.

"Time for a swim," said Helle, getting up.

"Alright," I said. "I'll sit here and look after the game."

Helle ran like a gazelle into the water. I recalled that she had done a lot of athletics when she was younger. She certainly had some kind of physical talent that I was sorely lacking.

I concentrated on the Scrabble board again. I could now prepare my next move in peace and quiet, try out a few possibilities, perhaps have a go with the letters. And if I was to find the right word, well then, there would be no harm in putting the letters down onto the board even though Helle was gone for a moment. I was sure we could trust each other that much. This was what I would call using time effectively.

I stared at the word she had just made. ANST.

ANST? What was that?

I was about to call out to her but she was too far out in the water to hear me. Perhaps she had put the words in the wrong order. I switched the first two letters. NAST. Nope. TANS? Not that either? STAN? Surely not? Here I was, trying to clear up the board, but to no avail. No matter what I did it just got worse and worse.

Haagen and Helle were playing catch out in the water. I noticed that he was surreptitiously staring at her breasts. I trusted that he was behaving himself. He was my friend, after all. Innocent until proved guilty and all that.

Then again, if he wasn't my friend, I would give his saxophone a beating it wouldn't forget. I could always super-glue the keys together. Now there was a tried and tested prank that never ceased to get a reaction.

He could look at Helle's breasts, that was fine by me. But he wasn't allowed to STARE. That was something completely different. Right now he was walking a very fine line. And if he tried to JUSTIFY it? Well, that'd mean he'd basically already crossed the line.

I got up and walked a few steps towards the beach.

I hadn't seen Higgins since we sat eating the sausages. I looked around in every direction and finally spotted him a bit further down the beach. He had collected a stack of driftwood in a pile. In another pile he'd assembled a variety of plastic cans and rubbish.

"All of this is mine," said Higgins when I walked over to where he was.

He positioned himself in front of the rubbish as if he was about to defend his wife and daughters from a band of horny highwaymen. Did he really think that I was about to go for him? My job was to explore the remainders of the language

41

our ancestors had left us. He surely knew that.

"Okay," I said.

"Mine. Just mine," insisted Higgins.

"Thanks for the sausages by the way, " I said.

To improve the atmosphere a bit I helped him carry the rubbish to the truck. An old Adidas jogging shoe put me in mind of summer nights under an open sky in the early nineteen seventies. Whether or not the shoe was mine I had no idea, but I sensibly kept my mouth shut.

"I'm going to start a new sculpture," said Higgins.

"Really?" I said.

"It's going to be called 'Worstward Ho'."

"Great title," I said.

"I stole it from Beckett," said Higgins.

The mention of Beckett made me think of birdhouses for some reason. I told Higgins about the progress I was making on my novel, and about the story of the birds that had disappeared. Higgins listened quietly, clearly interested.

When we got back to where the others were, Helle and Haagen had had enough of being in the water. Helle walked up to where we were and sat down beside me on the beach. I couldn't help but notice the drops of water that fell from her breasts. It occurred to me that they had got bigger lately, which was a shame as I liked them as they were. After all, I'm not the kind of man who thinks that breasts are better the bigger they are.

Helle told me all about her colleagues that had split up during the summer vacation whilst we ate supper that evening. She talked about the new kids in her class, and about her nephew who had gone over the top of his bike. He'd made the classic mistake of getting his front wheel caught up in the tramlines.

"He was lucky not to damage his head," said Helle.

"He might have learned something if he had," I said.

"What do you mean?" said Helle.

"When it comes to bikes and trams, I am completely on the side of trams," I said.

We had ended up in Helle's kitchen after a strenuous trip from Bygdøy. Higgins had suddenly realised that the lights on the truck weren't working so with the autumnal dusk descending, I had sat with a pocket torch shining the way in front of us whilst Higgins drove at snail's pace back to the city.

"You're talking rubbish again, Hobo," said Helle.

"It's not rubbish," I said. "Cyclists are almost as dangerous for the community as bad paintbrushes."

Admittedly, the conversation had got a bit side-tracked. I was more concerned about the tea cup I was drinking from. Wasn't this my favourite cup? It had the same pattern and colour – London Bridge in weak November sunshine. It also had the same little chip in it by the handle. But all the laws of physics said that this cup was safely placed in the kitchen cupboard of my own apartment.

"Apropos paintbrushes," I said. "When have you thought of making a start on the redecorating?"

"Not at this precise moment," said Helle, and got up.

"Wouldn't it be good to get it over with?" I said.

"Come on," said Helle.

"Can't we ask my parents to dinner one day?" asked Helle a bit later whilst we were lying in bed, naked, watching the late-night evening news.

Helle's parents were a subject I was happy to discuss at length. Whenever, wherever and even under the most unwelcome circumstances, I was happy to discuss these two friendly souls. On this occasion, however, I made out as if I was in deep concentration, totally focussed on what was happening on the TV screen and didn't hear what she said. It's a good technique and one to be recommended whenever you're in a fix. And that wasn't far from the truth at that very moment as the Hubbing-case was being discussed on TV. We'd both been interested in it for a considerable amount of time. A new-born baby had been found abandoned in the forest, partly covered by leaves. The police were hunting high and low to locate the mother but there was insufficient evidence to point in any particular direction. The police were appealing to the mother, who was no doubt under considerable pressure, given the situation, to come forward and seek help. No doubt a wide range of psychologists, psychiatrists, clergy and social workers were available to give her the support she needed.

The other main story on the news was about a crime writer who was suffering from a nasty bout of writer's block caused by his cat running away. He was reportedly spending everyday prostate on his sofa, thinking about his cat, unable to write a single word. A spokesman for his publisher pleaded with the public to be on the look-out for the cat because the writer still hadn't finished the manuscript he was working on. It should have been finished ages ago as it was supposed to be the main attraction in the coming edition of Book of the Month Club.

Helle was silent for a moment after the news had finished then repeated her question.

"When did you say?" I said.

"I didn't," replied Helle.

"No, well I suppose it's not that important then, is it?"

"What about Thursday?" said Helle.

"Why this Thursday?" I wondered.

"They're going away on Saturday," said Helle.

The next day I sat for ages at work going through an article about a man who bussed in loads of Swedes to a Norwegian shopping mall. The trip cost next to nothing, and it had been a success as the Swedes had found things cheaper, the man told the paper, than back home in Sweden. Particular bargains were to be had for things like a disposable lighter, a screwdriver or a stack of loo rolls left over from a military surplus outlet. On the trip the tourists were served rømmegrøt – Norwegian cream porridge – and a fruit drink and they sang all the way there and back. The article also revealed that there was even a toilet at the back of the coach!

It was an excellent idea and I decided to discuss it with Herman, my grocer, at the earliest opportunity. If it hadn't been for the fact that the article was full of grammatical catastrophes like BUSLOAD OF SWEDES CROSS BOREDOM, I would have rung up the journalist and given him a verbal pat on the back. Instead, I let it be.

Next up was the day's editorial. It wasn't often that I had the honour of going through the editorial several days in a row, so I took particular care to check the grammar and spelling. Reading through I understood immediately that the editor was out to point the finger at single mothers. Either they got too much or too little. As I read through I realised he seemed to be suggesting they had to get out and back into the workplace, although he didn't put it quite so overtly.

Suddenly something in the text caught my eye. I leaned closer to the screen. What was this? Did it really say what I thought it did? It really did! Holm had written: "We think that we're so good in everything in Norway."

GOOD IN? That's not right, Holm, I said to myself, and quickly changed the text, correcting it to "good at". I then carried on reading, now even more acutely on the look-out for other linguistic errors on Holm's part.

It was okay for a couple of sentences but then I stopped reading and started again from the beginning in order to get a really firm grasp of the content of the text and its linguistic nuances. It was one thing to spell and use words correctly; it was another if the correct spelling and words made each sentence full of ambiguities. I could see that Holm's editorial walked a dangerous line, verging on utter nonsense at times. Given that I was employed as a proofreader by Verdens Gang, it was my duty to ensure that he didn't cross that line and descend into troubled water.

After I had read the entire piece I adjudged it to be all over the place. This was unusual for Holm, who would have pointed out, without hesitation, that correct copy and content were two sides of the same coin. It really wasn't like him to write like this.

I picked up the telephone and dialled Holm's number. No one answered. A quick glance out of my window at the blue sky outside didn't help anyone pick up either. I checked the time. It was getting urgent. Time was of the essence.

It took me an hour to get the editorial up to scratch. By the time I was finally finished it was time to call it a day. Holm's office was completely dark and for a moment I wondered whether or not I should leave a message on his desk, gently reprimanding him for his sloppy work. But everyone can make a mistake from time to time, I thought, even Holm. My job was to tidy up the most serious misdemeanours.

Hjort didn't like me accusing him of stealing my a-ha records. He turned a nasty shade of red and looked about for something to throw at me. A serviette was too light, and a cocktail stick was obviously regarded as too dangerous. He was such a coward.

"Go on, throw it," I said. "He who throws things has a bad conscience!"

"You idiot," said Hjort.

"Maybe it was you who took my sofa as well?" I said, louder. "And what about my record player?"

Hjort disappeared to serve a guest over on the other side of the bar whilst I sat listening to "Hunting High and Low" which was playing in the background. I had indeed hunted high and low, I thought, but here was the thief, amongst my close circle of friends. A scoundrel who even had the audacity to use the stolen goods within earshot of the owner – yours truly! I was absolutely astounded.

Hjort glanced feverishly across at me whilst he poured two beers. I returned his gaze but with even more intensity. I was certain that I wasn't finished with that miscreant.

I suddenly noticed that people at their tables had turned to look at us. They were obviously keen to witness a verbal slanging-match that they could gossip about afterwards. It is quite nauseating to see how people in this city gossip behind people's backs. They are always twittering on about celebrities, neighbours and people they have been sexually involved with. I couldn't think of any other city in the world where they gossip more than in Oslo. I was certain of that.

Then the thief returned to where I was sitting and placed a

beer in front of me.

"Look at that," I said, "Drinking on the job?"

"It's for you," said Hjort.

"You're not going to blast yourself out of this tight spot with just a beer, Hjort," I said. "You'll need a cannon."

"Have a beer and calm down," he said.

"Calm down?" I said. "You're talking to the wrong man."

"Listen, I've got something to tell you," said Hjort.

So he was trying to butter me up with booze before he confessed? Well, if that was the case it was okay by me. I gulped down a large mouthful of beer and looked him right in the eyes.

"I'm all ears," I said.

"So you're wondering what happened to your sofa?" said Hjort.

"Is that all you have to say," I said.

"Listen up!" said Hjort.

"I'm listening. I'm listening," I said. "But nothing's happening. Just like those lads from a-ha, I don't like to waste my time with idle chit-chat. Morten, Magne and Pål WANTED something. They REACHED OUT for something. They were living in a dream, but reaching out for it at the same time. They really went for it."

"You're completely right," said Hjort.

What's actually going on here? I wondered after I left the Four Hens and walked up Frognerveien. Hjort had witnessed someone sneaking through the night with a sofa that bore a striking resemblance to mine. And if that wasn't enough, the two thieves had been decked out in orange boiler-suits, obviously in an attempt to appear as if they were acting in some kind of official capacity.

48

The information Hjort passed onto me didn't exactly improve my mood. Nevertheless, we made up on the spot and strengthened our until-now uncomplicated friendship. He lent me the café's CD of *Headlines and Deadlines* which would just about play on the crappy CD-player that someone had dumped in my apartment. He assured me in good faith that he had not touched a vinyl copy of *Hunting High and Low* since shagging a girl form Tårnåsen one time at the end of the eighties.

I shook my head despondently. Perhaps it's time to get away from my creature comforts, I thought. Go to London and try my luck there, maybe? I imagined myself wandering down Regent Street amongst people who didn't know who I was or what hopes and dreams were deep inside me. Not that I reproached them for it. They had their own dreams. Perhaps they wanted to be vets with their own TV show or car mechanics or maybe just meet the man or woman of their dreams and settle down in a little house an hour outside London? I imagined myself crossing London Bridge in the low September sunshine, on the way to my literary agent with my novel manuscript under my arm. I had translated the first couple of chapters into English and now I was ready to conquer the world.

There was a letter in my mail box from my publisher when I got back. It was a deeply prosaic communication enquiring whether I wished to purchase part or the entire remainder of my novel *The Letter*. If I indeed wanted to do so, I was instructed to fill in the accompanying form and return it by such and such a date.

I had been living under the misconception that I had already purchased the remaining stock but now I was unsure.

Had they had even more copies of my novel in their stockroom after all these years? A flash of pleasure shot through me. This was surely evidence that they had had belief in me, that like me they recognised the untapped potential in my early written work. This text was nothing but a preliminary sketch, a prologue to the writing of true merit that would appear not only in Norway but all around the world.

It was then that I caught sight of a couple of handwritten lines at the end of the letter:

This applies to a number of copies that we found whilst tidying up. Thought you might want to buy them, otherwise they'll be pulped.

Best wishes, Hildur Hansen.

The faint glimmer of pleasure quickly disappeared. Basically, they just wanted to sell me books that they were going to chuck out – Fair enough. I found a pen and scribbled on the sheet of paper:

SEND ME EVERY SINGLE SCRAP!

I stuffed the paper back in the envelope, put a stamp on it and went out immediately, putting it in the post box on the corner by Herman's store.

I stared at the shelves full of pasta sauce for an eternity. Finally, Herman came over and put his hand on my shoulder.

"Sorry," he said. "It'll be here next week."

"Next week?" I bellowed. "Damn it!"

My patience had run out. It was one thing that his wiener sausages varied by several centimetres in length within the same packet, but it was another thing not to be able to get hold of a jar of pasta sauce at a month's notice. I decided there was no way I was going to tell him about my idea of bussing in a coach load of Swedes. He could read Verdens Gang himself.

My anger surprised both of us and we stood there, staring at each other. Then I sat down on a beer crate and sighed.

"It's hot, isn't it?" said Herman.

"It is," I said.

"It's the heat, you know?" said Herman.

"Is it?"

"It builds up," said Herman.

"To what?" I wanted to know.

"It's going to thunder," said Herman.

That's what he thought! Or maybe it was just something he'd rattled off to calm me down? Did he have any idea what he was talking about? There were too many so-called weather prophets going about scaring the life out of people. In that instant I imagined a rainstorm washing cars away down the manholes in the road, and driving the moose into the forest. After the rain it turned icy cold and a new ice age was just around the corner.

"By the way, do you still cycle?" wondered Herman.

"No," I said.

"It's basically the tramlines that cause problems," said Herman.

"So they say," I said.

Holm was standing by the window when I entered. He had his hands behind his back and looked determined, as if he'd made a decision. On his desk was a copy of the day's edition of Verdens Gang open at page two. It was the page that included his own editorial. So he was one of those people who read their own work!

I hummed quietly to myself as I sat down in the visitor's chair.

"How's it going, Highbrow?" he asked.

"No complaints," I said.

"Are you happy here at Verdens Gang?"

It was a question that I had barely asked myself. I tilted my chair backwards a bit, thinking about it. I had been working for the paper for years. It was an important part of my life.

"Yes, absolutely," I said.

"How long have you worked here?" said Holm.

"Well, let me see..." I thought for a moment. "Won't it be thirteen years this coming spring?"

"Don't ask me," said Holm.

Either he didn't like the heat or he was having a bad day; he was acting very surly. I decided it would be best to patiently wait for him to get to the point.

Holm turned his back to me and stared out of the window. There was nothing happening out there but I supposed he could be following a piece of dust across the sky. As for me, I looked at my hands, which had spots of green paint on them. Where on earth had they come from? It was easy to scrape them off with my nails and I reminded myself every cloud has a silver lining.

I had been hard at work with a follow-up article about a certain male writer who had writer's block when Holm rang. The reason for the writer's struggle was that the writer's cat had disappeared. Now several crime fiction experts had declared that the situation was grave. The cat had to be located before something serious happened. The journalist was also one of those who suffer from the incessant need to use REALLY in every context: REALLY good at football. REALLY good at this and REALLY good at that. It irritated me immensely, as well as evoking a general sense of sadness on my part concerning the sorry state the Norwegian language was in these days. Everything was going one way – down the pan. It was at this point that the editor rang and I dragged myself away from the screen on my desk. I made my way through the editorial section where the evening shift had just started to collect the threads together for what would be tomorrow's headline article.

"What do you think about my editorials?" Holm inquired from the window where he was standing.

"Well..." I hesitated.

"Go on, let's hear it," he encouraged.

"To be quite honest I rarely read them," I said.

"Really?" said Holm.

He turned around and looked at me, his smile quickly vanishing and being replaced by an extremely serious and slightly aggrieved look which made me feel quite uncomfortable.

"It's often just enough to read the headline," I explained. "Then you get an idea of where it's going."

"Now I understand," said Holm, and sat down at his desk.

It was at this point that I realised he'd made a series of vigourous annotations in his editorial piece as he'd read it. The masses of red ink looked like a meteor of criticism had exploded in the article, consuming the entire paper and even parts of his desk.

It can be like that sometimes, I thought, when you regret what you've written. It was news to me, however, that Holm was such a hothead. He usually seemed so calm and self-controlled, oozing a sense of authority but with the ability to cut through the crap whenever necessary. If I could have given him a word of advice then and there I would have told him that what's done is done. He needed to keep his chin up and look straight ahead, instead of devoting time to something he couldn't change.

"As far as I understand, you were on the corrections desk yesterday, weren't you?" he said.

"Yesterday?" I said, after a moment's consideration.

"The person on the desk copy-edits the editorial, right?" said Holm.

"Yes, exactly. That's how it is," I said.

"There is some wording I don't recognise here, Highbrow," said Holm. "There are things here I didn't write. For example: 'Single mothers are our era's sacred cows, living off the spilt milk of the State'."

"But you were the one that wrote that," I said.

"Absolutely not," said Holm. "I wrote: 'many single parents are dependent on support in order to get by'."

There was a message on my answering machine from Helle when I got back to my office. She'd called to remind me of our meeting at the Four Hens after work. I was slightly taken aback. Why was she nagging? We always met at the Four Hens on Thursdays! She didn't need to chivvy me along like a little child.

I kicked the wastepaper basket so hard it flew through the air and lay on its side in one corner of the room. There was something about Helle's voice that irritated me. It was mellow and almost tender, as if she had just remembered something from childhood that she wanted to share with me. Her favourite story, perhaps, about how she found a bird in the forest that she took home and kept in a shoe box for a whole week? No, thank you very much!

I sat down and stared into my computer screen. The article about the writer who had lost his cat would have to carry on without me. But I didn't give a damn. I packed up a few personal belongings and took the lift down to the ground floor. There was a mirror in the lift and as I glanced at my reflection I noticed that my curly hair still had a bounce to it, despite the inlets being carved out on either side of my forehead.

On Akersgata the heat was more oppressive than ever, and in Lille Grensen the people I saw were looking decidedly hot and bothered as they trudged along.

The blue blue sky lay like a heavy blanket over the city.

Haagen was sitting in the bar chatting with Hjort when I got to the Four Hens. He glanced over at me but quickly turned back to his conversation whilst I walked around the bar looking for Helle. She wasn't at the girls' table in the corner or sitting at the regular's table by the window. If I was quick I could sneak a swift beer before she got here.

I didn't get it. She'd never bothered to take the slightest interest in what I drank. So why now? Especially now that my body's need for liquid refreshment was equal to the distance between it and the nearest beer tap.

"Over here," roared a voice.

Higgins lay under the regular's table fiddling with something, although I couldn't see what. He was wearing his trusty old Hawaiian shirt which he usually reserved for special occasions and what I recognised to be his favourite Adidas running shoe on his right foot. On his left was a Puma trainer of more recent vintage.

"What on earth are you doing down there?" I asked.

"Looking for used drinking straws," said Higgins.

"What's the point of that?" I said.

"Drinking-straw art is the in thing in New York right now," said Higgins.

"As if!" I said, regretting it almost immediately.

"Look, there's one over there!" I said and pointed towards the wall.

Higgins crawled towards it and then stood up with a yellow straw in his hand.

"Perfect!" said Higgins.

"Anyone seen Helle?" I asked as we approached the bar.

"She's in the toilet," said Haagen.

"If you want to know what she's doing in there you'll have to go and look for yourself," said Hjort.

I stood and looked over in the direction of the toilets and as I did so she came out, wearing her black leather jacket and something that vaguely resembled a tiny trouser-dress underneath.

"Is the kitchen starting to look nice?" I said as I kissed her.

"Yes," said Helle.

"Is everything okay?" I wondered.

"It's slow going," she said.

"It's the weather," I told her.

"Really?" she said.

"Herman says it's building up to something," I said.

I wondered if I should tell her about my job. Of course I should, I said to myself. Only I just had to wait a bit, that's all.

It started to get quite crowded. People were moving around the smoke-filled bar in search of someone to chat to. Hjort had obviously switched off the air-conditioning hours ago. Still, it was all I could do to follow the conversations which had slowly shifted from being rather objective to being utterly subjective and rambling.

"I make my best sculptures when I'm wearing really tight underwear," admitted Higgins.

"Huh?" said Haagen, just as he was making eye contact with a woman over by the bar. She was the spitting image of a Hilde, Herborg or Halldis. It seemed the attraction was mutual as neither could tear their gaze away from the other.

"My sculptures lose their edge when I work with my balls dangling in the wind," said Higgins. "They need structure and support for their life."

"In!" I called across the table.

"In what?" said Higgins.

"They need structure and support IN their life," I said.

Higgins, on the other hand, admitted: "I can't stand fish balls in white sauce."

We all sat thinking about this as we drank and smoked, keeping our knees tightly closed in the hope of putting off the next trip to the toilet by a few more minutes. I looked up and saw some bloke making his way through the bar with a chair balanced on his head. He was heading for our table. I had seen him before. He was an acquaintance of Haagen. It was the famous and rather gruesome Hagbart, who had played the triangle or the recorder on some record or other in the eighties. He squeezed his chair in between Haagen and Helle and interrupted.

"I thought I heard someone mention fish balls?" he said.

"We're talking about underpants," said Haagen.

"I prefer not to wear any," said Hagbart, winking at Helle.

What was this bloke up to? I moved closer to Helle and held her hand. She squeezed my hand in return, which settled my nerves somewhat. But then it occurred to me that if she was interested in him, she wouldn't avoid holding my hand so then I felt I had to speak up.

"Played a lot of triangle lately have we?" I said.

"Triangle?" said Hagbart.

"Yes, I thought you played the triangle," I said. "Or was it the castanets?"

Hagbart laughed, smiling, and explained that he played bass. Perhaps we had heard him playing fretless bass on the most recent Hubert and the Hamsters record?

Nope, none of us had! But it didn't seem to affect Hagbart much; he just leaned forward and said in a low voice: "It's all about keeping a really even tempo."

And he stared right into Helle's eyes as he said this.

I glanced at his hands. They were hairy and horrible.

"Really?" I said.

"Really," said Hagbart.

What was going on? Was this idiot sitting there, flirting with Helle? Or maybe he was REALLY flirting with Helle. Even worse.

"What are you getting at?" Hagbart said to me.

"He's a proof-reader at Verdens Gang," said Helle and she sounded so content that I felt like a hook she hung her hat on.

It was at that point I suddenly realised I didn't have a job anymore. The thought made me get up quickly from my chair. All at once it was bloody hot inside the bar! Had they put the heating on already? I was clammy and perspiring and the air was heavy and tough like an old toffee.

I went outside for some air. A police patrol car drove slowly past. I nodded in a bloke-ish sort of way to the policemen in the car and glanced up toward the heavens. By God, a cloud had appeared high up in the sky. Although it wasn't black, it was at least very dark. It's about time I went home, I figured.

As I went back into the bar I bumped into Haagen who was wandering around. He took me to one side and, shoving his bearded face right in my direction, began to talk. No matter what it took, he wanted to tell me all about his latest project with Higgins. It was something he really needed to get out to the people. I didn't get it all. It involved bread or fish or something. Or a bouncy castle that turned up on Saturdays in sparsely populated areas! Some touring was involved, either way. Something where there was a lot of money to be made. And then he started talking about the weather of all things. The winter was coming, he told me, and revealed that he had an AGREEMENT with someone or other. Was it me he meant? I didn't have a clue what he was going on about. The word MONEY however evoked something in my consciousness. Either that or it went in one ear and out the other.

Helle didn't seem to have noticed that I had been away. I took her hand in mine again and signalled that I wanted to leave. But she remained sitting, glistening in the heat, her sweaty hand in mine. So I freed myself again and went out to the toilet.

It occurred to me that lawlessness had gone too far in this city, as I eased the pressure in my bladder. People took things into their own hands. Especially when it came to erotica. Some people seemed to think it was just a case of helping yourself to what ever you wanted, without showing any respect to anyone else. They gorged themselves as if it was the first time they'd ever been in a sweetshop and thought everything was free. But sooner or later the bill always arrives. It was something the most progressive of us were aware of.

When I came back from the toilets I sat down, moving restlessly around on my chair, trying to catch Helle's attention afresh. She sat there leaning towards Hagbart, listening to his never-ending monologue about how you tuned a bass guitar with a northerly wind blowing at you and the temperature dipping below zero degrees Celsius. As far as I could gather the first step involved taking off your mittens but the whole procedure got lost amongst the clinking and murmuring of the drinkers frequenting the Four Hens.

I tugged Helle's blouse, first gently and then harder, right until she slapped my hand away and leaned closer to her partner at the table. I followed suit and with deliberate determination blew in her ear. It was something that ought to remind her of romantic trips, early in our relationship, to the mountain tops of Telemark. But this didn't work either so I decided to play my final hand and hummed our own private melody. If she didn't get it now, it would be on her own back.

"Can you cut that out?" said Helle, then turned away again.

She looked indignant as if I was an irritating fly, bothering her. And in that instant I felt like some creepy insect who bowed his head and blushed in front of the entire audience.

I stared at Hagbart's hands. They roamed across the table with considerable frequency and for some reason made me think of a couple of kilos of smoked sausages. They were hairy too. All the same, this man seemed to be charming Helle! There was something about her expression: it radiated a delicious glow. And it had fuck all to do with me, a voice deep inside my chest screamed!

I looked about. All the others were busy. They were yapping away, drinking, showing pictures of their wives and children to strangers they would never meet again.

Where was help when you really needed it, I wondered?

Where was authority and the clergy?

Where were the POLICE?

At that moment I saw four or five of Hagbart's sausages move from the table and in the general direction of Helle's left thigh.

I stood up and shoved my chair back.

"There's a fly on the ceiling!" I shouted.

Everyone looked at me. Hagbart and Helle and Haagen, who had finally managed to light a cigar after what had been an immense struggle.

"Up there," I said.

I pointed up to the ceiling.

"Don't you believe me?" I said mockingly, staring right at Hagbart, who looked momentarily confused, before he let his pig's trotters down again onto Helle's thigh.

"Look for yourself," I said.

With one swift punch I smacked Hagbart exactly where I intended, right in his gut. He sank down onto his knees, letting out a long 'Arrr' from his lips. The sound was followed by a waft of tapas, liquorice drops and cheap beer from some or other east-end Oslo dive.

"You deserved that," I said.

Meanwhile, Helle yelled something incomprehensible. Then she stood up and looked both surprised and concerned at me, before she bent down on to her knees to pamper her new little friend.

Hagbart remained sitting for a moment, holding his stomach. I made the most of this interlude to take a swig of beer, waiting for him to get up. It took considerable time, however, as he stayed down and then started looking around for small change on the floor.

It was typical of someone from Sunnmøre, I thought. But it was okay by me. I had time to think of something else. My novel-project, for example. The great literary tome, exploring the great themes of life and death and love, as well as a smattering about the construction of birdhouses.

When, at last, Hagbart began to get up, fumbling like an old man, I kneed him in the face so hard that they would hear it all the way over at Ørsta dental surgery.

Two policemen decked out in leather jackets were standing behind me when I turned around. Trouble was *policemen* didn't fit: one of them was a genuine woman.

"You're late," I said.

"Perhaps we should take a trip down to the station, High-brow?" said the policeman.

So they knew my name! I was impressed. Rumours spread quickly in this city. Without a doubt, I really was a name in the literary community.

Both officers looked like they'd stepped right out of a detective novel.

"That won't be necessary," I said. "The man you're looking for is lying right there."

I shoved the tip of my shoe into the side of Hagbart, who was lying on the ground groaning like a child that had banged his knee. He needed to realise that he had to shut up until I had finished talking to these honourable upstanding representatives of authority.

"I think we really should take a trip to the station, I really do," the officer said, taking a step closer.

He spoke just like my father. This, in turn, made me think of my father. He would have been proud to see me now. A son who really punched his way forward in life.

The police woman sat next to me the whole trip down to the

station. She was a very nice girl by the name of Hansson.

"Is it Mr Highbrow, the writer, I have the pleasure of meeting?" said Hansson, almost blushing.

"It certainly is!" I exclaimed.

"Oh, I've read *The Letter*," said Hansson.

"I could see at once that you were someone who really knows their literature," I said.

"I'm always at the library," said Hansson.

"There are worse places to frequent," I said.

"I have a penchant for Pessoa's poetry," said Hansson.

"Pessoa?" I said.

" 'I am nothing. I shall always be nothing. I can only want to be nothing. Apart from this, I have in me all the dreams in the world'," quoted Hansson.

" 'The Tobacconist' by Álvaro de Campos?" I guessed.

"Exactly," said Hansson.

The poem in question was one of Pessoa's rather cack-handed pieces, but I thought it was better to keep my mouth shut about it at that particular moment.

I lay on the floor of my cell listening to the noise from that night's arrests. Someone called out for God, someone wanted mother and another wanted a cigarette. No one asked for pizza, for example, or pasta with Dolmio sauce. I thought about something the great Rilke had shared; namely, that if a poet was in some prison, he would still have his childhood to draw on: "that jewel beyond all price, that treasure house of memories?"

But how did that help me now? I was a tormented man. A man shut inside a cell, imagining how Helle had left with Hagbart after I had left the Four Hens. I imagined her treating his sores as if they were grenade wounds from The Winter War.

And after that it would be home for a romp in the sack.

I could see the scene played out in front of my eyes; Helle on top of the idiot, as he played bass with her breasts. And all the time I was lying there in danger of being charged, and just because I was defending my lawfully won rights. It was too much to bear.

There was only one thing to do right now: to create literature based on my experience. At least then I could earn a couple of kroner from the experience. But was there any paper to be had in this cell no larger than a toilet? It was decidedly anti-art in here. You couldn't say this was where art thrived under the cosh. You could shit without a paper and pen, but you couldn't write sonnets, I told myself, looking around the cell for something to write on.

I eventually fell asleep in the early hours of the morning, and dreamt that I was carried down to the ocean on a blow-up mattress. It was comfortable enough until the waves got too big. I realised I was on the point of losing control, somewhere out there in the North Sea. I woke with a start and was met by a pair of friendly eyes.

"How's it going?" said Hansson.

"I had a dreadful nightmare," I said.

"It almost serves you right," said Hansson. "You understand now that you can't go around behaving like you did last night, Highbrow?"

"I dunno," I said.

"Next time, you're going to have to control your temper," said Hansson.

"I suppose I'll have to," I said.

She helped me get up, straightened my jacket and led me out into the corridor and into an office. Once there, my watch was returned to me. It was ten-past eight.

"I also write a bit," said Hansson.

"Do you?" I said.

"Mostly lyric poetry," said Hansson. She then sketched out her approach to poetry, albeit in potted form: Poetic technique was, for her, everything that wasn't to do with her job. Except football, that is.

"I understand," I said. "My advice is to not reveal everything to your reader. Let them do a bit of the work themselves."

"Thanks for the tip," said Hansson.

I felt a cold breeze as soon as I stepped outside of the police station. Had autumn arrived whilst I'd been under arrest? Autumn, with its bubbling lamb and cabbage casseroles and angry blasts of wind? Autumn, with its fine days and never-ending rain? The sense of joy increased in me like sap in a seedling. I had been down for the count momentarily, but now I was ready to fight on.

The sense of joy didn't last long, however. As soon as I felt the rays of morning sunshine, I realised that today was going to be warmer than the previous day. My dream of cooler days, alas, had to remain a dream for the time being.

If anyone had asked a couple of weeks earlier if I was interested in refuse trucks, I would have laughed at them. I might even have been a little snide. Now, however, I was rather fascinated by the refuse trucks which stood parked alongside the pavement. My fascination wasn't diminished either by the sight of a particularly intriguing sign on the side of one such vehicle: *POETRY EXPRESS* - YOU RING FOR IT, WE BRING IT.

Higgins sat in the driving seat tying straws together. He stared at me as if assessing my mental and physical state. His conclusion must have been positive because, after a brief pause, he continued with what he was doing. That was one thing I liked about Higgins. He was as busy as a bee. Goal-orientated and everready. Every free moment for him was a potential brick in the construction of art's grand temple.

"They seem mainly to make yellow straws," he said after I climbed in next to him. "It's a theory I'm on the point of proving scientifically."

"What's your hypothesis?" I asked.

"That Oslo is full of yellow drinking-straws," said Higgins.

His mobile phone rang. He listened carefully, simultaneously finishing off his meticulous work with the straws and putting them under the seat.

"We have to go," said Higgins, once he had finished his conversation. "Haagen needs help."

I could hear the sound of faint music coming from the grave of Hjalmar Holst-Humperdinck, the wholesaler. A whiny, somewhat dampened sound of a saxophone pushed its way between all the mumbling widows sat on their knees, planting things on the graves of their wilted husbands.

Haagen was laying down with his saxophone in his sleeping bag. He was practicising "Öppna Landskap", which echoed across the cemetery and over the gravestones.

"How's it going?" I asked.

"As long as I am in bed with my beloved, no harm will come to me," said Haagen.

"That's a fine position to take," I said. "But how on earth did you manage to zip yourself in your sleeping bag like that?"

I sat down defeated on the gravestone, ready to shake Haagen's relationship to his ten thumbs.

"YOU can just shut up," said Haagen.

"Oops," I said. "Have I managed to step on your toes already this early in the morning?"

"Firstly, you physically attack the finest bassist I have ever got my hands on," said Haagen. "And secondly, you leave it to others to take your lady home."

68

"My lady?" I said.

"She's very upset," said Haagen.

"Really?" I snapped. "So she's upset, is she? What's she upset about?"

"That's not so easy to say," said Haagen.

"Isn't it?" I said.

Haagen remained still and we sat listening as a train thundered past and Higgins tried to undo the zip on the sleeping-bag. If Haagen thought that I was going to force him to tell me about Helle's emotional state, then he was sadly mistaken. I had much more to do than to listen to what my ex-girlfriend was up to in her spare time. I had a career to build.

The zip opened and Haagen pushed his saxophone through and put it down on one side. Then he began to get dressed whilst still inside the bag. He had a unique technique which I admired and had never got close to.

Although I knew what Haagen was getting at with his commentary, I wasn't the first writer who had hit out now and then, if the truth be told. Perhaps I ought to remind him that Hemingway regularly needed to get into a fist fight? Or a certain Dadaist who at the start of the last century ran around Zurich with a loaded pistol trying to shoot his rival. I presumably had been casting pearls before swine.

Higgins got going with frying eggs and bacon on Haagen's camp stove while Haagen busied himself with a few knee-bends and fixing his tie which had been hanging on a branch.

"It's time to give up the outdoor life," said Haagen, as we each sat on a gravestone eating.

"Have you had enough of it?" I inquired.

"You're the one to ask!" said Haagen.

"Aren't I allowed to ask, perhaps?" I said.

"Ask if you want," said Haagen. "Whether or not you get an answer is another question altogether."

He was in a damned funny mood! Here I was, just released from a police cell, hanging out with Haagen in the middle of nowhere, and he had nothing better to do than piss all over me with his attitude.

"What IS your problem?" I wondered.

"Autumn's just around the corner," said Haagen. "And I don't even want to think about what's right after that."

"Take it one step at a time," I said.

"We need a goal and a roof over our heads, Hobo! *The Poetry Express* could be the beginning of something big. Poetry for the people! Wrapped in sweet tones and visual art!"

Haagen was suddenly speaking with authority. He was speaking like a leader who points the way out of a roadblock for his congregation of old people, women and children. Higgins sat there nodding, looking up at the sky.

"We all need to move on," he said.

On the way back we passed a couple of containers. Higgins stopped and found two steel lamps and an office chair that he wanted to take with him. Haagen found an old, crooked music stand which, with a bit of good will, could be used to dry socks on. After that we carried on to Higgins' studio where we found the occasion to sneak a look at "Worstward Ho".

Higgins had used driftwood for the base of the sculpture whilst the other parts were attached as points of emphasis or associative elements; the large watering can was mounted on the long trunk like a kind of "stomach" whilst "my" jogging shoe was like some kind of "beak". But from what I knew of Higgins, there were a thousand ways of interpreting an art work like this. It was a case of anything goes.

70

"Do you think I should paint it?" asked Higgins as we stood there.

"Dunno," I said.

"It would be an encroachment on the material itself," said Higgins. "But a careful touch of colour might give it a necessary lift."

"I agree," said Haagen.

"Agree about what?" said Higgins.

"What about a bit of red on the stomach?" I said.

"What stomach?" said Higgins. "Who said anything about a stomach?"

"It looks like a stomach," I said.

Whilst Higgins and Haagen prepared a more detailed presentation of the *Poetry Express* Project, I took a stroll around the studio. Apart from the mess, which covered every inch of the floor, it was clean and tidy. Well, tidy in the sense that there were two orange boiler suits hanging on a peg.

"Nice," I said. "Do you know what Hjort said? That he saw two men in suits like that carrying my sofa across the city."

"When?" said Haagen.

"In the middle of the night," I replied.

Haagen and Higgins were a bit too involved in their own stuff to participate in conversation about a wandering sofa or so it seemed. They had spread out an enormous drawing on a stained bit of empty floor and motioned me over to have a look.

I noticed that my answer machine was blinking "new message" as soon as I entered the apartment. Blink blink, blink blink. Two quick blinks meant that there were two new messages waiting for me. They could be two short messages or two long messages. It could be a silent breath from the past. Someone that wanted to remain anonymous, perhaps. Or it could be a really unexpected message, uttered in a loud and clear voice: "Get on the first plane to London!" Perhaps my agent had read my manuscript and wanted to discuss terms at his office immediately.

I pressed the button.

"Hi, it's Helle here. You disappeared so quickly yesterday. I wondered if everything was okay."

Disappeared so quickly yesterday! That's a nice way to put it after leaving me in the lurch.

"Hello. It's Helle again. Can you give me a call? I've invited Mum and Dad to dinner on Thursday. I'm thinking of making Boeuf Bourguignon. Does that sound okay? And there's something I need to talk to you about."

Does that sound okay? No, it does not! It sounds dreadfully hurtful, actually. And this thing she wanted to talk to me about. What was that all about? What hadn't we talked about? She had to be much clearer than that. I was thinking clearly with a capital C. As clear as the mountain springs that wolves drink from, bits of dead sheep hanging from the corners of their mouths.

I imagined how the conversation was going to go. In fact, it was actually easier to imagine that than how my protagonist was going to build a birdhouse.

"I want you to know that I really like you," was what Helle wanted to say.

"I really like you," she would say.

"I hear what you're saying," I would reply.

"We can still be friends," she would add.

"Can we?" I would ask.

"Of course," she would say.

And then I would lie and tell her that the pasta sauce was boiling over in the kitchen and, yes, I would tell her, it's actually splashing up the walls and ceiling, I'd say, and before I knew it I'd be getting bogged down in a long description of the trials and tribulations of Jesus.

Then Helle would laugh gently at the other end of the line.

"Take good care of yourself," she would say and I would hurry to be the first to hang up.

I tried to picture her; first, her dark hair which she had cut really short with a fringe like an Egyptian beauty; then her smile (which had bloody well turned out to be as fake as I don't know what!); then the way she walked, which I imagined was how Egyptian women moved thousands of years ago with water pots on their head, wearing no underwear. I bet Egyptian men back then didn't complain: it must have been a massive turn on.

I didn't really appreciate my thoughts conjuring up a sexual element like that. After all, I wasn't exactly in the mood for erotica having spent the night in the slammer. Besides, it brought my spiritual side back down to earth with a bump. Not that I had nothing against whores or Madonna or any-

73

thing. As long as they could be trusted. But on this evidence, it seemed women were not to be trusted. Any charlatan with money to burn and the gift of the gab could talk his way into a woman's bed.

Helle had deeply disappointed me.

She'd sold our love for a handful of pieces of silver.

That was far too cheap.

The boxes filled with books were heavy. I dragged them into the living-room and opened them. There it was! Some really early copies of *The Letter*! They were a few copies that had been left to gather dust on the east side of Oslo. "Dust" was too mild a turn of phrase, perhaps. "Crap" was much better. Some copies had that well-known FROM THE PUBLISHER stamp on them here and there.

The amount of boxes and other rubbish that was gathering in my apartment was now quite considerable and I decided I had to take immediate measures if I wasn't going to get shut in. I basically had to get my act together and clear space for myself.

One current drawback with the apartment, however, was the lack of a sofa and coffee table. I needed somewhere to put my feet up when I took off my socks and wanted to air my toes during my little breaks in between writing. I needed somewhere to roll beer bottles whilst watching *Norge Rundt* – Around Norway – on TV. I needed a solid table with space for a large cream cake and plates in case people like Haagen, Higgins or Hjort couldn't resist popping in to visit certain people on their birthday. But this was heading down a rocky road...

All that stuff about birthday visits wasn't exactly that important right now, I determined, as I started forming a layer of *Berry Picking* on the parquet floor. Someone had deemed it necessary for me to be born on July 15 and at that point the city was deserted. Everyone had gone south or strawberry picking in Lier. You had to be grateful if you were born in the autumn, I thought. Just like the lads in a-ha. And look what that had led to!

I used a whole box of poetry to complete the first and most important layer. The sonnets were so permeated with life lived that they'd be able to hold the rest of the table in place, I thought.

The most difficult thing about the next stage was to figure out how I was going to stack *The Letter* – lengthwise or widthwise – or possibly in a pattern, pointing inwards to the room. It took almost an hour figuring this out but as I later told Haagen: "It was worth it!"

When I was finished, I collapsed on the bed and sighed contentedly after an honest day's work.

I had done something really quite useful.

I didn't spend long resting on my laurels, however. No, no one can say that. A flash of inspiration sent me shooting out of bed, scrutinizing the bookshelves. The most recent conversation with Helle about Olaf Bull had sowed a seed of doubt in my mind about how much she could be relied upon when it came to literature. Thus far I had kept a clear distinction between my feelings and the purely academic. I was of the opinion that if people were rotten scoundrels, but only in certain moral situations, it didn't mean that they were entirely lost ships in others. But now it was time to ascertain whether I had been far too naive and trusting on the subject of literature as far as Helle was concerned.

I took Olaf Bull's collected poems and short stories down from the shelf and positioned myself by the window. With the help of the table of contents at the back of the book I quickly discovered that "Sommerens Forlis" was neither in *New Po-*

ems or *The Stars*, but in *Poems and Short Stories* from 1916.

No, this wasn't some misunderstanding. Helle had deliberately misled me. Although I had ceased to believe in her love for me, I had up until this moment at least had full confidence in her linguistic and literary competence. Disgruntled, I ripped the book in two and threw it out of the window.

Next it was the Scrabble. To get rid of my own, personal Scrabble set was much more painful; nevertheless, I deemed it entirely necessary if I were to move on. I opened the rubbish chute to find that the game was too large to throw into it. I had to squeeze the cardboard box into the opening. A few of the letters fell out and down the chute: lonely letters in free fall. And it seemed as if I heard them land with their own unique sound: A! B! G! X!

Having completed the necessary tidying up, I felt considerably better and ready to tackle my novel. I already had many important scenes in place but it was putting it all together that was the problem. Besides, I hadn't thought about trying to get away with a flash-fiction novel, written in fragments of keywords scattered like beacons on a mountain top. Literary success required the writer to guide the reader from page to page. Large empty spaces that gave the north-wind space to frolic was forbidden. This time I was completely focused on reaching out to as wide an audience as possible, although naturally I wasn't prepared to compromise my own integrity as a writer. I was certain that when I finally produced this masterpiece, I would instantly become established among the literary elite.

Of course, I didn't just mean the Norwegian literary elite. I was thinking much more global than that. There were literary agents out there in the big wide world and it was imperative that I was able to get in touch with those kinds of people. They would be my industrious moles, digging my path to success in the global literary landscape.

I put *Headlines and Deadlines* on and "Take On Me" began to blast from the speakers. Immediately I was gripped by a spurt of inspiration and spontaneously began writing a scene where the protagonist realises that he is part of something much larger than he'd previously thought. After his travels in the East, where he sporadically visited nomads' tents and spent solitary days under a sweltering sun, life wanted him in a more demanding situation. Wasn't it the case that he could just dream the birds into existence – without any other result than being woken in the morning by birdsong in major and minor? Or did he perhaps take on overall responsibility for the little feathered ones? Questions stacked up as I wrote, but given that I was one of those people that liked questions more than answers, I let them remain unanswered until my creative self had come up with a suggestion through the process of writing.

The writing zipped along smoothly through the entire length of "Take On Me" and halfway through "Cry Wolf". Then a couple of practical issues regarding the construction of birdhouses began to divert my attention. I was aware that there were a variety of techniques that could be employed when constructing birdhouses and I lacked practical experience in this field to be able to write convincingly about it. So there was no other option than to do a bit of research.

Someone knocked at the door.

I remained seated.

If I had any hope of creating something that was of significance for humanity, I couldn't be available at all times like some kind of hot-dog stand.

I picked up a pencil and sharpened it to a fine point, wondering whether Hemingway ever got up to open the door when he was in the middle of writing. Probably not. I didn't even know how widespread doorbells were during the years after the First World War. For all I knew they might have stuck to door knockers or simply used the old-fashioned method of rapping one's knuckles on the door in the hope of being heard.

Suddenly, I heard a rustling in the letter-box. I jumped up and walked towards the door. People were getting more and more impertinent. No doubt this was a veritable scoundrel on my doorstep who wouldn't take no for an answer. In one swift move, I whipped open the door and looked to see who was there.

Helle stood bent over in the process or trying to put an envelope through my letter-box. It was an importunately intimate action, it occurred to me, utterly devoid of any respect for my privacy.

"This is a private dwelling," I said.

Helle stood up and looked at me questioningly, one hand on her back like an old lady who had spent too long sleeping on a bad mattress.

"I didn't know you were in!" she said.

"Where else would I be?" I said.

"At work," said Helle.

If she was going to be so finicky about details such as whether I was working at Akersgata or at home or on the moon for that matter, she should put her own house in order.

"It disappoints me that you are so deceptive," I said.

"What on earth do you mean?" Helle asked.

"You know full well what I mean," I said. "Does Bull mean anything to you?"

Helle tried to sneak a look past my shoulder and into my apartment. Yeah, I suppose a few bits and bobs were a bit different since she'd been there last. For all I cared she could stand there looking at nothing of any interest before I continued with the interrogation. While I was waiting, I scrutinized her closely, now that I had her close at hand. She was pale and looked terrible. TERRIBLE. But, I supposed, that was the consequence of shagging all night and not drinking sufficient water.

"Do you mean Olaf Bull?" said Helle.

"For example," I said. "Although admittedly there are plenty of other members of the Bull clan. There's Brynjulf Bull and Trygve Bull to name two for starters."

There was something about Helle's expression. She wanted to say something or other but I wasn't finished. Not even close. And then I realised that she was wearing a ring that I had no recollection of having previously ever seen. It was thin and shiny and reminded me of an engagement or wedding ring. Clearly, things were moving extremely quickly.

"You said the other day that "Sommerens Forlis" was in *New Poems*. But that's utter tosh," I said. "Imagine that you would lie about such a thing!"

I realised at that moment, much to my horror, that I was actually standing there with tears in my eyes. Where on earth had they come from? You learned something new everyday. That was now quite apparent.

"Can I sit down?" said Helle.

"Impossible," I said. "Someone has stolen my sofa. Besides I AM WORKING."

"There's something I have to say to you," said Helle.

"I understand. I understand," I said.

"Are you coming home soon?" Helle asked me.

"Home?" I said. "As an artist, I am perfectly at home in my own body. You can meet me when I am ready. But right now I am closed for the day!"

I ushered her out of the doorway and closed the door again. To be entirely sure, I put the latch down, locking the door. I then returned to my work. On the floor, however, was the letter Helle had pushed through the letter box.

Although I knew what it would say, I bent down to open it. It was one thing to know the truth yourself but it was another to have someone else shove it in your face. Given my preoccupation with semantic niceties, I was intrigued, however, to see how Helle had expressed herself. If, for example, she had made the slightest grammatical error I would possess something that could be used against her should we ever meet on the street or in a store in the future.

"I can see things are not going well for you," I would then say.

"How?" she would wonder.

"You've started spelling 'unfortunately' without an 'e'."

"No I haven't," she would protest.

"Oh yes you have," I would tell her.

And then I would simply smile, leaving her there, confused and scared on the pavement or possibly between the shelves in the store, and I would go back to my apartment and my imminent breakthrough as a writer.

Herman had finally got in some Dolmio with garlic and mush-rooms. He'd ordered a few extra jars on my account and put them aside in the storeroom at the back. I was grateful to him for all eternity. Finally, I was back on track – at least nutrition-ally. It was the alpha and omega for the task in front of me.

"Doesn't the pasta sit like a rock in your stomach?" asked Herman.

"No, that's an old myth," I said.

"The older the better," said Herman.

"Athletes eat a lot of pasta," I said. "That should be proof enough."

Herman shrugged and answered the phone. I understood that it was his aunt, Hulda Høilund, calling because he came over all gushing and accommodating. It was painful to listen to.

"Cabbage it is then," said Herman. "And tonic water?"

When he'd finished talking to his aunt, he asked me: "Do you have anything to do?"

"Yes," I said.

"Come over here," said Herman.

We went out the back. There was the delivery bicycle al-though it still said "Herman's Corn" instead of "Herman's Cor-ner" in big, black letters on a blue background. There was also a nice cover to protect the supplies from the rain or attacking crows and other thieving beggars.

"Basically, you just peddle and make sure you steer in the right direction," said Herman.

"That's two things at once," I said.

"If you include the tramlines it'll be four," said Herman.

A bit later I struggled out of Herman's yard on the old bicycle. In the delivery basket lay the cabbage and tonic water for Mrs Høilund and Helle's letter was in the back pocket of my trousers, burning like an old flame that wouldn't quite go out. Mrs Høilund probably had a very nice rubbish bin that would gratefully receive a letter from a deceitful lover and hide it away in its cosy embrace. Both the letter and I were now on our way.

Perhaps, I decided, it wasn't so bad cycling after all. I felt a hint of freedom as I carefully navigated the tramlines along Frognerveien before heading out along a tramline-free route all the way up to Kirkeveien by Frogner Stadium. Mrs Høilund lived by the cemetery and although it was a tough ride up the hill to Volvat, I wasn't going to get into any self-punishing crap; I was ready for the fight.

Questions began to bother me again. Did I have to leave the country to reach my true potential? To be recognised in the first place for who I really was? Couldn't I just as well manage with nine square meters in London or New York as thirty in Oslo? Although the idea wasn't exactly appealing, it made sense. Nothing tied me to Norway anymore. My love had been shattered into a "thousand pieces" as the Swedish singer Björn Afzelius had so precisely put it. Actually, my love wasn't in 'pieces'; it was more like dust which the wind was carrying to the ocean along with the sea gulls and birch pollen. My job was also but a mere memory now. Soon I would grow listless, no longer reacting to the linguistic decline of this northern country. Wasn't it enough of a reason to get away to a country where the language's riches were held in esteem and culture was the cornerstone of a nation's self-worth? Didn't, for example, Joseph Conrad start writing in English as an adult? He established himself as a major force in British literature! And not forgetting Morten, Magne and Pål, who left Norway behind and set off for England? And then my thoughts turned to my friends: Haagen, Higgins and Hjort. There were a couple of things that grated there too.

I took a breather by Ringhuset. I had, after all, not sat on a bicycle since the time I voted for the Social Liberal Party during the local government elections at the end of the seventies. Or to put it another way, my bum was really saddle sore, my body ached in four or five other places and my breathing wasn't as it should be.

I placed my hands on my buttocks and massaged each cheek. The only thing I achieved with this, though, was to rip Helle's letter out of my pocket and send it blowing across the asphalt. As far as I was concerned it might as well just stay there. Then again, it was a matter of privacy. The idiot that found it might want to use it against me some day. I picked up the envelope and resolutely opened it.

Helle had unusually beautiful handwriting. I had never had a single problem following the loops and curls and punctuation that was all in its proper place. I didn't quite get what the letter said. And if there were any spelling mistakes, well I wasn't in any fit state to tell. I rubbed my eyes and re-read it:

Dear Hobo,
I'm just leaving you a note in case you come here during the course of the day. We need to talk soon. I am pregnant.
Your Helle

Mrs Høilund had been an attractive woman in her younger days. She was pretty attractive now taking into consideration the fact she was in her nineties. She was wearing a silk dressing-gown with embroidered hearts, butterflies and flowers. On her feet were a pair of thick socks. She quickly looked me up and down before disappearing into the house with small, shuffling steps.

"Put the box on the table," she called from the living-room.

The kitchen was light and very pleasant but the only food or drink I could see on show were three bottles of red wine standing on the kitchen bench. Next to them was an ivory corkscrew decorated with tiny prints of London Bridge. It was an impressive piece of handiwork.

"I just have to listen to a bit of the French news," said Mrs Høilund.

"Do that," I called back.

She was lying on the sofa with her ear pressed against a small transistor radio when I entered the living room. The room was furnished with antiques and the walls were decked with various kinds of art. Along the walls were empty wine bottles in long, neat rows. I detected at once that here indeed was a woman who had a taste for beauty and spiritual values. Or perhaps it was Mr Høilund who had brought all these objects into the house? There was no trace of him, though, so I decided to give his wife the benefit of the doubt.

On a small table there was a pile of books. I lifted them carefully, looking at each in turn. It came as no surprise to find a copy of Hubert Humpelfinger's wretched *Erogenous Zones in the Middle Ages* amongst the books. I dropped it as if I'd accidently picked up a dead rat.

"Shhh!" snapped Mrs Høilund. "I'm listening."

"I'm very sorry, madam," I said.

"They've got Victor Hugo in the studio," said Mrs Høilund. "He's just published a new novel."

"He's dead!" I said.

"Really?" said Mrs Høilund, looking at me rather sceptically. "Are we going to be difficult today?"

"No, no, not at all," I said.

"Could you be so kind as to go into the kitchen and open my bottles of red wine for me?" Mrs Høilund said.

I walked back to the kitchen and willingly got on with the task in hand. I liked the feeling of doing something useful, of being a miniscule cog in the wheel that went by the name of CARING FOR THE ELDERLY. A mechanism that admittedly struggled from time to time, but was driven by a gang of diligent and engaging people like myself.

The corks in the bottles were impossible to budge for some reason and it didn't help matters that Mrs Høilund was shouting incomprehensible instructions from the living-room. Each bottle was to be marked when it was half-empty because she consumed exactly half a bottle of wine every day. Also, each day had to be marked in such a way that the upper part of the bottle was labelled Wednesday and the bottom part Thursday. Otherwise mix-ups would easily occur, which was quite understandable. Each cork was to be unscrewed from the corkscrew and pushed one centimetre down into the top of the bottle after it had been opened.

When I was done I looked in on the living-room and figured that the lady of the house was still listening to the radio. A classical concert was now on, having replaced the news. Lying there, no doubt remembering old flames, she looked delighted. All the pain was washed away and there was nothing but happiness left, so I decided to leave her in peace and quiet for a bit.

On the kitchen wall there were pictures of Herman when he was a child. First as a baby on his aunt's knee, then on a fishing trip as a teenager. There was also a picture of him wearing his graduation cap as a twenty-year old. It was a pretty nice progression through the years but I missed the obligatory picture in the bath which seems to have become a standard feature of Western culture. Herman would have stared right into the camera with a rubber duck in one hand and a plastic boat in the other.

The pictures reminded me of Helle's letter. Now what was it we needed to "talk about"? It certainly wasn't to discuss the weather. Helle wasn't the kind of person to bother about whether it was wind or rain. She took everything as it came and made the best of things. Philological quibbling wasn't important for Helle either anymore, that was certain. When it came down to it she was interested in other things. I thought about the way she'd signed her letter to me: "Your Helle". It stank worse than forty garbage trucks.

So she was pregnant! Okay. She wasn't exactly the first woman in the country who had unwillingly got herself knocked up. In fact, there's quite a long tradition of it in Norway. The Norwegian sociologist Eilert Sundt noted as much in his research back in the 1800s. He discovered so much immorality in the small towns and villages across the country that he almost gave up. If Helle wanted to talk to someone about it, she should talk to the father of her child. Hagbart, probably. The man whose hands were like pig's trotters.

Thinking about Helle's letter had made my mouth rather dry. This coincided with the horrific realisation that one of the bottles of red wine on Mrs Høilund's kitchen table was fuller than the others. This was an irregularity that Mrs Høilund would no doubt seize upon and would in all likelihood inform Herman over the phone. So I opened the bottle and took a generous swig.

"What on earth are you doing, young man?"

Mrs Høilund stood in the doorway looking at me. She was pale and could hardly stand on her own two feet. Her beady eyes glared at me.

"Oh, I'm just adjusting the water level," I said.

"I want a massage now," said Mrs Høilund.

I remained sitting on the bike outside Mrs Høilund's house, gathering my strength. Thankfully it was mostly downhill on the way back, but I was not used to cycling. Besides, the visit to Mrs Høilund had drained me, both physically and mentally.

I stared up at the road. A hill led up to the area at the bottom of Holmenkollåsen. The asphalt was covered by damp leaves. On both sides of the road were expensive houses with large gardens and long driveways – they probably required copious amounts of shovelling to keep the snow at bay during the winter months of the year. I thanked my lucky stars that I lived in an apartment.

Was it right of me to have left Mrs Høilund without ensuring that everything was okay? She didn't look particularly all right. But Herman had told me she was the sort who was destined to live until she was a hundred, so I relied upon his good judgement. He knew better than me about those sort of things.

It was beyond me how that old lady would finish off all that tonic water during the course of a week. Not to mention all the cabbage. But I realised that this kind of job required a rather large dose of discretion. These questions did not concern me.

A couple appeared at the top of the hill pushing a baby-buggy. They were laughing, mucking about. I suspected that they were two happy first-time parents enjoying a walk in the autumn sunshine. A little family out and about. Dad's remembered the baby-bottle and extra diapers. Mum's wrapped up the little bundle of joy against the winter that's waiting to pounce from behind every garden bush.

Their laughter grew nearer. The dad leaned over the baby, tickling it, and laughed. It struck me that it was as if the baby was just something to tease. As far as I was concerned, children were bloody hard work. Still, I wondered whether there was anything good to say about them at all? I couldn't immediately think of anything, but I realised I shouldn't come to any quick conclusion: I should give children a chance.

I leaned forward over the handlebars, watching the couple with the child come closer and closer. The woman had dark hair and was thirty-something and the man was boyish and very lanky, seemingly without a care in the world.

It suddenly struck me that this is ONE thing positive about children: they're undoubtedly the best opponents to face at Scrabble. They're easy to beat and it's amusing to trick them. I remembered the couple of times I'd played Scrabble with Helle's nephew several years ago. It had been a pleasant way to pass the time. What was his name again? Håkon? Harald? It was something regal in any case.

The couple with the baby reached the corner where I was philosophising, sitting on the bike. The woman didn't look Norwegian and she was small next to the man. Something about them told me that they were just visiting. That was why they were so cheerful, I thought, and understood why. A family who've ended up in Norway for a couple of days would naturally be pretty cheerful at the thought that they would soon be leaving the country again. They obviously freely and willingly embraced this invention that was Norway, sauntering along, tourists in this peaceful heavenly place.

As they walked past the man turned and glanced at me, and as he did so our eyes met.

The last drop of air squealed out of the bicycle wheel with a whistle that reminded me of the sound slithering reptiles make in the grass of the African savannah. It was this kind of sound that made my colleague, the Danish novelist Karen Blixen, leave Kenya for her home in Denmark. The whistling-sound nagged away in the background continually, ruining her creativity. On the verge of acute writer's block, Blixen packed her bags and headed back north.

I was standing right in the middle of a crossroads with the rim of my wheel trapped in a tramline and two or three impatient motorists behind me. What was I to do? Plead for God to help me? Sing a hymn? I was a fair way from Herman's store, in need of help, and I felt abandoned like a tiny child left all alone in the forest to die. The cars began to beep their horns behind me. With one enormous tug I wrenched the wheel free and pulled myself out of the firing line. As it turned out, I was near Helle's school and something inside me sent me heading off on a detour in her direction to wish her a final fond farewell. As I cycled I felt like an air balloon climbing up to the heavens, tied only by a thread to my homecountry. The unexpected was just around the corner. Tomorrow I could be in London, Kenya or even New York!

When I got to the school gate I saw Helle come out of the sports hall together with a boy. He looked a complete twat with his trousers hanging down around his knees, a beanie pulled down over his ears and a massive plaster on one arm. Helle was wearing the same old summer dress that I'd liked in the past, but now, as I stood there, it struck me as ugly and in utterly bad taste.

What they had been doing in the sports hall was a good question. Helle was a well-qualified philologist, without a doubt, but despite her considerable performances on the sports track when she was younger, she had rarely put a foot inside a sports hall since then.

The pair of them walked slowly across the school yard, talking and laughing the entire time. Wasn't Helle looking a tad unusually stressed? A bit red in the face, perhaps? As if she'd just played leapfrog or climbed the rope? Or maybe she'd been jogging in an attempt to keep fit?

Maybe something else had occurred? The very thought made me shake my head slowly. Was this the real father of her child and not Hagbart? Or were they still both strong candidates for the title? The boy, who disappeared into the main school building, was old enough to be Helle's son! I shivered. I would never have imagined that Helle could fall to such depths. Or perhaps I noticed things without really picking up on how serious things were? Yes, I believed that might well be the case. Then again, it's always easier to see something with hindsight. Still, I was lucky to have escaped the clutches of this woman.

Herman was talking with Mrs Høilund when I got back to the store. They were obviously talking about the Hubbing-case as Herman mentioned the words FOREST, the CHILD and the MOTHER. They then changed topic and each seemed to express their concern about the weather. The outlook wasn't good as it predicted the heatwave would continue, bringing with it a risk of forest fire. If it continued in this manner, we would miss out on the most charming stage of autumn, I thought. Victor Hugo wasn't mentioned at all.

"It went well, I hear?" said Herman.

"Absolutely wonderful;" I said. "Your aunt is a charming creature."

"She is, isn't she?" said Herman.

"But you're bike needs sorting," I said.

"The tramlines?" he said.

"What else?" I said.

Herman opened the till and settled in cash. He must really care about Mrs Høilund because he gave me more than a bit of loose change.

"Can I count on you next time?" said Herman quietly.

"Why not?" I replied.

Someone had ruined my construction. Half the sofa was gone and the table was lower than before. It was flattering, of course, that someone was interested in books like *The Letter* and *Berry Picking,* but was this really the way to go about showing it? At the end of the day I was an obliging man who willingly gave copies of his books to reading circles for the poor or single mothers. But there were rules to abide by in society; you wrote a letter, made a phone call or at the very least rang the doorbell and asked before you went and took something.

I got undressed and went into the bathroom. There comes a time when a man just has to cut through everything and wash his problems down the plug hole. And that time was now, I told myself. But as soon as I stood in the shower, I started to worry about other things. The green flecks of paint had spread to other parts of my body. They had crawled down from my hands to my elbows and onto my chest. A few red specks partly covered the green ones which struck me as even more serious. They looked like bloody sores and were much harder to get off.

If it didn't stop soon I would have to go to the doctor's. The doctor was, of course, someone I usually tried to avoid; however, if it was serious enough I would swallow my medicine and go to the health centre. From this moment on, I told myself, I needed to stop being so careless with my body.

Once out of the shower and dry, I realised someone had called. It was Helle, nagging about the dinner with her parents again. Was she really so dense? She was wondering if she should serve Sicilian pasta with prawns, olives and bacon. She ended the call by asking, rather hopefully: "Have you read my letter?"

NOOOOO! I yelled at the telephone and opened the wardrobe with a veritable yank. This woman was really beginning to irritate me. What kind of nonsense was this? I was well aware that she was probably operating with two possible fathers to her unborn child, namely HAGBART and COCKY WHIPPER-SNAPPER WITH THE PLASTER. She should concentrate on them and leave this particular hard-working artist alone.

I took a moment to survey the contents of my wardrobe. The top shelf was earmarked for underwear. It was a deep and wide shelf with plenty of space for boxer shorts and more tightly fitting briefs but right now it was empty. The second to top shelf had, according to tradition, been used for socks. Socks were something I was particularly concerned about. I preferred them to be black and made of cotton terry. Alas, that shelf was also empty. In fact, my entire wardrobe was empty! It gaped at me like a hungry shark.

I flopped down onto the bed. What a day it had been! I was worn out and so, snuggling under my duvet, I decided to put my novel on hold until I'd recovered my strength.

The magazine under my pillow was completely new to me. It was an old copy of guitar magazine PLECTRUM, in New Norwegian instead of the more usual Bokmål, that had somehow found its way into my bed along with a copy of the glossy tabloid SAX WITH THE EX. This rather turgid publication was about celebrities, sex and playing the saxophone. PLECTRUM, on the other hand, contained informative interviews with guitar heroes and the very best kind of pop artists.

I had thought less and less about Helle during the last hour. I simply lay in bed dozing, fantasising about nice things like tiny delicate canapés served at massive book launches in New York or London. Soon Helle would be nothing but a memory, banished to the inner dwellings of my mind.

I flicked through the guitar magazine. A major interview done in conjunction with the release of Savoy's new album caught my attention. It opened with the following line: *When Pål Waaktaar was a young man, dreaming of being a pop star, he never supposed he would one day be called Savoy.*

Nicely put, I thought. He surely didn't know that just as he didn't know that he would go on to become one of the major composers of the second half of the twentieth century? Or perhaps he really KNEW it? Did really talented people know on some physical level, deep inside them, that one day they would be great? I took a moment to ask myself this. YES, it really was so.

My gaze fell upon the picture of Pål Waaktaar, his hair recently coloured and done in a bit of a comb-over. But who was the woman next to him? The small, cute, dark-haired little thing.

I read the text under the picture: Lauren Savoy.

So THIS was Lauren!

Sure, I'd seen pictures of her before but I hadn't really got a sense of her personality. In this picture she revealed a totally different side of herself. As I lay there I sensed that Pål had gone through fire and rain for this girl from Boston. She had recently given him a son, August, but called Augie, according to the press. He had written a couple of hundred songs for her, showering her with confidences the rest of us would have kept to ourselves. Not that this was disheartening in any way.

And I began to understand that for some people love was a really massive and beautiful thing worth fighting for. That some people really were willing to hunt high and low for the person they could really love. I hummed "Hunting High and Low" and translated a few lines into Norwegian as I went:

Searching high and low
Oh, there's no limit
To how far I can go

Hmm? Was that what he really sang? It didn't sound as good in Norwegian. It's one thing to be head over heels in love with someone but another thing to croon your love for someone like a wimp at the microphone. I am yours, do what you want with me! "There's no end to the lengths I'll go". Maybe the correct Norwegian translation was: "*no limits to how far I can travel*"? If that was the case, it sounded like a travelling song.

I got out of the bed and began to walk backwards and forwards with the magazine in my hand while thinking about what I had done earlier that day. There was something familiar about the couple with the buggy I'd seen outside Mrs Høilund's. Suddenly, a thought began to grow stronger and stronger inside me until I just had to get the telephone book and start looking. Under "Savoy" the only thing listed was the Hotel Savoy and I couldn't imagine those two in the bar with their baby buggy and extra diapers, slightly tipsy, laughing and ready for all kinds of debauchery. But what made me even think that they'd purchased their own place to live in Oslo? In this tired city full of tired people? Wasn't New York good enough anymore?

I looked again at the picture. There was no doubt. It was Lauren and Pål I had seen with Augie, safe and sound in the buggy. They'd laughed and just as they'd walked past me, Pål had turned to look at me for a moment. He threw his head back as he laughed and let his gaze fall momentarily on me.

The two turtledoves had then carried on their amusing little stroll, their laughter rippling over lilac trees and rhododendron bushes that had shed their blossom long ago and rubbish bins which would soon be covered in a thin layer of rime.

I sensed a strength and joy seeping through my body, through my legs, my arms, across my chest and up to my head. I had met Pål Waaktaar! I had looked straight into the eyes of Pål Waaktaar! And I had felt a shock jolt through my body as if for a second I was momentarily connected to an electric network with an unknown power. The power of the massively talented. It was the power of those who created art that would last for eternity.

I've never really cared about the lyrics of pop songs. Either the melody gets me or it doesn't. As far as I'm concerned, they can sing about what ever they want as long as they don't depress me! As far as I am concerned the whole purpose of pop music is to drown out all the world's misery. Music is all about helping you keep your dreams alive!

All the same, perhaps I had done Waaktaar and a-ha an injustice by not listening to their lyrics? I decided to make an honest attempt to make up for what I had neglected. I got comfortable in bed with my notebook on my knees and a pencil in my hand. "Take On Me" was spinning in the CD-player.

The title seemed to work on first hearing. TAKE ON ME literally translates as *"touch on me"* in Norwegian. But what about TAKE ME ON? *Touch me on*? It sounds forced and rather odd. On the other hand, it was one of the things that embodied the linguistic dexterity of Waaktaar's texts. An Englishman, American or an Australian probably wouldn't say it like that! Then again, it wasn't a native-English speaker who had written it. It was a shy young lad from Manglerud, Norway.

Touch on Me

Speaking away
I don't know what to talk
I will talk anyway

Today is yet another one to find you.
Shying away (Look it up in the dictionary!)
I'll be coming to pick up your love, OK?

Touch on me (touch on me)
Touch me on (touch me on)
I'll be gone
In a couple of days

So unnecessary to comment
I'm jumbled up
But that's me, stumbling along
Slowly realising that life is OK
Repeat what I say
It's no better to be secure than regret

Touch on me (touch on me)
Touch me on (touch me on)
I'll be gone
In a couple of days

I had now finished with my rough translation of "Take on Me" so it was about time to get down to set about capturing the nuances of the language. It was, of course, tempting to let it stay like that, and avoid submerging myself in word games. But my conscience forced me to investigate the myriad interpretations that could be made of the lyrics. So I got up and went across to the bookcase and found my English-Norwegian dictionary and looked up TAKE ON. It turned out it means a variety of things: *to take on, to get on with, to take over, to undertake*. I double-checked with my American dictionary of slang, which said: *to react strongly, to make a noise, to ravage or lay waste to*. It wasn't mind-shatteringly enlightening but I began to realise there were contours of deeper meaning to the phrase. For starters, there was a soupcon of neediness in the line. A sense of needing to be acknowledged, to BE SEEN!

I'll be gone in a DAAAAYYY, Harket sings in falsetto in the original version. It was tantamount to a demand to seize the opportunity, Carpe diem, seize the day. We live in this room right at this moment; we have to live so look at me NOOOOW. And take on me NOOOOOW!

No, I had to avoid touch for a moment and try instead with looking.

See on Me

Speaking away
I don't know what to talk
I will talk anyway
Today is yet another to find you.
Shying away
I'll be coming to pick up your love, OK?

See on me
See me on
I'll be gone
In a couple of days

There was a knock on my window just after midnight. I had put my translation on hold for a while and was in the kitchen preparing a bit of supper. A moment earlier someone had rung the door and I'd wondered if it was Helle trying again. Perhaps she thought I needed to hear that we were JUST GOOD FRIENDS again before I hit the sack. Now she'd get to hear what I thought about the whole thing and stuck my head out into the dark.

"I'm WORKING!" I bellowed.

"Fine," said Haagen.

"Actually I'm asleep," I said.

"I think you should make up your mind," said Haagen. "Watch out!"

He threw a black bin liner through my window and climbed in after it. This was a clear violation of my attempts to keep a certain amount of peace and quiet about me, so I tried to hold his head down, as if attempting to drown a pet in the bath. It was useless though. He barged his way in with the help of his saxophone.

"Smells good!" said Haagen, once he was fully inside my kitchen. "What's cooking?"

"Pasta," I said.

"And what's this?" said Haagen, sticking his nose into the jar of Dolmio sauce.

"Garlic and mushroom sauce."

"I brought along a few knick knacks," said Haagen, pointing out into the darkness.

I looked through the window again. Down on the street was a chest of drawers, a bean-bag and a bag of rubbish.

"Seriously, Haagen," I said. "There's no room for all that crap in here."

"Come on outside," said Haagen.

"What's it like being unemployed?" said Haagen a bit later on. We had carried his things into my apartment and were sitting in bed listening to the washing machine that was on in the kitchen.

Had the rumours spread so quickly? I couldn't remember telling anyone that I had lost my job. Besides, I wasn't unemployed. I was working on my novel now.

"I might well be in the mood to discuss the term 'work' with you," I said. "Have you, for example, thought about the enormous amount of work that is undertaken by trees on a daily basis in this country. The tons of water that are heaved about IN SPITE of the power of gravity, nourishment that's transported by countless transitions from the earth via the roots and then out to the tips of the leaves. Or what about the work animals do? And I don't mean ants in particular. What about, for example, the squirrel that collects his acorns?"

"It happens that I think of squirrels," said Haagen.

"What is it that you want?" I said.

"Are you prepared for the show at the Four Hens on Thursday?" said Haagen.

"Well, ready as I'll ever be," I said.

"You're not really interested in participating now, are you?" wondered Haagen.

"No, not really," I said.

"It's not really your style," said Haagen.

"What do you mean by that?"

"You sit here on your high horse and fart all on your lonesome," said Haagen.

"I'm writing a novel," I said.

"Who isn't writing a novel?" said Haagen vaguely.

"What do you mean by that?" I wanted to know.

"How's it going with you and Helle?" said Haagen.

I didn't like the way Haagen kept suddenly changing the subject. Just as I thought we were segueing into an exciting discussion about the art of novel-writing and working with big, complex texts, he started going on about Helle. Completely out of context. This wasn't good for my health.

"Helle's doing fine and sends her greetings," I said. "She's pregnant."

"I know," said Haagen.

"Really?" I said.

"Any man with the slightest bit of education can see when a woman is pregnant," said Haagen.

"You're kidding," I said.

"The question is rather to what extent you figure in the picture," said Haagen.

"That's easy. I'm totally out of the picture. I'm not even in a tiny corner of the picture. If you were a betting man I'd say that it's odds on Hagbart is the father. If you want a second bet, I'd put your money on a kid at her school. You can't mistake him. He's got a massive plaster on his arm.

"Harald?" said Haagen, somewhat shocked.

"You simply ask and ask," I said.

Haagen rolled his eyes and then pointed at my hand. On one finger there was a thin metal ring, presumably of gold, which I had never seen before. It was reminiscent of an engagement ring, the kind of ring people give each other to show off the fact that they've managed to pick up some partner after years of wandering in the desert of Oslo's nightlife.

"Congratulations on the new ring," he said.

"Whatever," I said.

"What's that all about then?" said Haagen.

"No idea," I said and tried to pull the ring off my finger but it was useless. My fingers were swollen after all the cycling.

"It really pisses me off that people throw around rings like that," I said.

"Be careful!" said Haagen. "You need all the fingers you've got."

What on earth was he going on about? It sounded like some kind of subtext that trembled under the surface when Haagen was talking. It was incredibly tiring that he went on like that.

"What's this then?" he said, picking up my notebook with the translation of "Take on Me" on it.

"A folk song I've translated from Slovakian," I said.

"Can't you just admit that a-ha are totally passé?" said Haagen, with a rather patronising glare.

"Wrong," I said. "a-ha are going places they've never been!"

Haagen shook his head and continued reading. He carried on reading, then threw the notebook down.

"I had quite forgotten how deeply in need of physical contact young boys are in Manglerud," said Haagen. "Magne Furuholmen and Pål Waaktaar sat there once upon a time playing music, clapping along in time with a metronome, closeted in a basement. Maybe they gave each other a bit of a massage to help with a stiff neck. Or healing by placing their hands on each other? Touch me!"

"I think Asker is more likely, and Morten Harket!" I said, to show just how off track he really was.

" 'Take on Me' is typical of Waaktaar," said Haagen. "Pubescent notes from his diary wrapped in a synthetic cream of rhythmic frippery."

I got out of the bed and began to circle the room like a fly buzzing about. Haagen's provincial petty-mindedness and know-it-all attitude was so incredibly evident. He was an idiot. A numbskull. A dick-head who would never manage to drag himself out into the open landscape as it was riddled with white currants and other berries.

"No wonder the record company wanted a stack of horny girls around the boys during the filming of their first video," continued Haagen. "They were undoubtedly a flock of mummy's boys who gave off a strong whiff of homosexuality."

"Now you're not being nice," I said. "The need to be touched isn't unusual for humans or animals. Not mentioning the need *to* touch."

"But what about hitting, a bit of a smack, punching someone on the nose and that sort of stuff?" said Haagen. "Isn't 'Take on Me' really a subtle demand to use more violence?"

The look Haagen gave me made me realise that he found my entire interest in a-ha decidedly unhealthy. With that I wavered and fell back into the aesthetics of touch with the more literal interpretation of the expression TAKE ON. And I thought about the incident at the Four Hens. Could I ignore the fact that "Take on Me" was in the back of my head somewhere, not forgetting the back of a certain Hagbart's head either? Yes, wasn't it the case that "Take on Me" was the background music for this scene, drowning it with its deft rhythm?

I understood at once that we were in a place where boundaries were easily broken. There is an invisible boundary around each and every person, I thought. For some people it's a half-metre around the body; for others, the boundary isn't a physical thing at all: it's a psychological thing. Hit me, by all means, but don't step on my blue suede shoes, as Elvis would have said. And of course, he's not thinking about getting dirty, but establishing a psychological boundary figuratively through a pair of shoes.

"a-ha and Pål Waaktaar are the biggest thing to have happened to Norwegian pop music since Ole Bull melted the hearts of women at concert arenas around the world," I suddenly said. "And you just sit there with a saxophone in your gob, thinking that you know the answer to everything. There are still too few people in this country with the same recklessness, self-belief and who give a fuck about stepping outside the comfort zone as they did. a-ha, as far as I'm concerned, deserve to be celebrated unreservedly. Hip Hip Hurrah! Hurrah! Hurrah!

"You're a nice lad, Hobo," said Haagen.

"It just makes me nauseous all this cynicism about people who really want to do something," I carried on. "I've felt it first hand and know quite a lot about the effect it's had on a-ha too. I think the lads themselves can take it, but it really pisses me off having to listen to all this cynicism. It says something about this cesspit we call Norway. a-ha are a bunch of intelligent, very talented people doing their own thing. But is that ever good enough? No. Journalists know best. They've been patronising and petty-minded and asking stupid questions from morning to night. Nothing else was expected in a shit hole like Norway where people have to kiss someone up the ass to get their face in the local paper."

Haagen looked tired. Had I used too many long sentences? It often got like that when I got carried away.

The next morning I awoke on the floor in my apartment and remembered that Haagen had kicked me out of bed during the course of the night. He was still in bed, lying there alone with his saxophone, spread out.

It was okay because it gave me the chance to lie there with my hands behind my head and look up at the ceiling and collect my thoughts from the previous day's conversation.

All the crap Haagen had rattled off about Waaktaar and Furuholmen's childhood in Manglerud had to be put down as pure ignorance. Haagen was, otherwise, a rather educated gentleman who could tell amusing anecdotes about the saxophonist Charlie Parker. Like the one, for example, about how Parker was a popular ladies' man in New York because he had very strong tongue muscles. On many an occasion he had to take them home to demonstrate just how strong it really was. Often he was tempted to say "No", but his reputation went before him and, well, he had to live up to it!

As soon as Haagen was awake, I instructed him to get dressed and took him out onto the street under the pretext of "going for a morning walk". I wanted to make it quite clear to him that there was no way we could co-operate on a joint-venture whilst he maintained the same attitude towards Waaktaar and a-ha as he had demonstrated the previous evening. He simply had to be prepared to change his mind.

When we rounded the corner I saw the Tårnåsen bus appear at the end of Bygdøy Allé. I grabbed hold of Haagen and quickly got him across the road to the bus stop. Here was an opportunity for both of us to increase our knowledge of terraced-houses in Manglerud.

We were soon sitting on the bus. Haagen was positively surprised by my initiative and excited to be out on a trip. It was probably because it reminded him of trips in the west of Norway. As we rode along he rocked backwards and forwards in his seat the whole time, trying to look out of the window. He didn't want to miss a thing; for example, the momentary uncertainty of which way the bus driver was going to take at a crossroads. Neither of us had a clue where Tårnåsen actually was, but figured it was just a stone's throw from the centre of Manglerud. But I had to double-check with the bus driver.

"Does this bus stop at Manglerud?" I asked.

"Manglerud?" said the bus driver.

"Yes," I said.

"What do you want to do there?" said the bus driver.

I told him what I was going to do. About the terraced houses and the dreams that grew amidst the basements there. About social democracy's yearning children.

"Those terraced houses in Manglerud are infamous," said the bus driver. "I've lived at Ryen myself and count myself lucky that I got out in time."

He then told me that he had inherited his parents' smallholding in Hadeland and had commuted ever since.

"I am a happy man," he said.

I took his answer to mean 'No'; nevertheless, I didn't give up.

"Is it a long detour?" I asked.

"To Manglerud?" said the bus driver.

"Yes," I said.

"Far too long. Besides, I'm running late," he said, and put his foot down heavily on the accelerator.

When I got back to my seat Haagen had fallen asleep. It hurt seeing him like this. I'd dragged him out of bed to take him to Manglerud. Trouble was, now we were heading in the wrong direction. He hadn't even had any breakfast either.

By Stortinget – the Norwegian parliament – a familiar figure got onto the bus. It was my ex-editor, Holm, out and about on a trip. Was he doing one of his rare reports? Or was something else on the programme? I wondered, shifting in my seat.

The answer soon became apparent as Holm hoisted his golf bag up on to the seat next to him. The pair of them sat there like an old married couple on a bus trip to Strömstad.

I woke Haagen as we approached the central train station. It would be a shame if he missed this part of the journey. He looked about him confused and wondered if we were in Balestrand. I strongly denied this. We were nowhere near the west coast of Norway!

If the truth be told, I was too concerned with catching a glimpse of Mangelrud to be bothered by Haagen. Manglerud was somewhere up on the left, but the bus took a sharp turn to the right and shuddered its way out into the provinces alongside Bunnefjorden.

"Beautiful," mumbled Haagen, who promptly dosed off again.

A few minutes later, amidst what looked like the countryside with vegetation on both sides of the road, the bus suddenly pulled over. Holm got up, glanced over at us at the back and got off the bus. There was no house, pavement or even a trail to be seen on either side of the road. As the bus drove off, we saw Holm carrying his golf clubs through the thicket and into the forest.

"I'm hungry," complained Haagen, slouched deep down in his seat.

"We'll have something to eat at Tårnåsen," I told him.

"Tårnåsen?" said Haagen. "Weren't we going to Manglerud?"

"Absolutely," I said.

After a while the area became more built up again with a few buildings and we caught sight of terraced houses. This prompted Haagen to revive and he got up to have a better look. If we didn't make it to Manglerud, perhaps there was something worth seeing in Tårnåsen?

The bus stopped and we got off rowdily, full of expectation. After the first couple of excited steps we stood still, looking about. The only thing of any interest was a supermarket with a café.

Haagen looked disappointed. Still, remaining optimistic, he came up with a creative suggestion.

"I have to go to the bog," he said.

"Me too," I said.

The café was deserted except for an old lady who sat doing the crossword. Otherwise there was no one in sight; not even behind the counter or in the toilets. Haagen shut himself in one of the toilets whilst I was quickly done. I went into the store. The man behind the till was sitting down, asleep with his arms wrapped around it like it was a pillow. Anyone who could steal the cash till at Tårnåsen without waking him would have to be really good!

My gaze fell upon the newspaper rack. Dagbladet's headline was as uninspiring as usual. The crime fiction writer still hadn't found his cat. Both his publishers and Book Club were still extremely concerned about the gravity of the situation.

As I turned my gaze towards Verdens Gang I thought for a moment that it said GV, but after closer inspection I realised it said VG as usual. Unfortunately, the headline was horrific. CHILD'S MTHER FOOND, it said.

I flinched. Wasn't there anyone in the office checking the text? Still, why should I care? It didn't bother me. But then a terrifying thought occurred to me: what if there was someone or other out there who didn't know that I'd stopped working for the paper? Maybe they were thinking why is HOBO HIGH-BROW letting all this crap through his net? The thought was utterly depressing.

I left the store and started pacing around in front of the door. I didn't feel in the least bit sorry for Holm. He'd brought it on himself.

On the way back we sat in silence, each of us lost in our own thoughts. Even though I was a bit disappointed, at least we knew a bit more about life in this little part of the world. Now we could go home again and continue get on with our lives, I thought, without having to give Tårnåsen another thought for the remainder. And if anyone ever asked about Tårnåsen, we could say: "Did you say Tårnåsen? I've been there. It's a hovel."

I am, if the truth be told, not the kind of writer who enjoys doing research. I tend to focus on things that have come across my path, either through reading or my experience in the real world. To look up a place or information so I can write about it is something I only do in an absolute emergency, and never without my dark glasses or my collar pulled up.

It was now time, though, to find out more about the technical side of building a birdhouse. It was an emergency and I had to bite the bullet and consult the literature on the subject, otherwise I wouldn't be able to make any progress on my novel. Luckily, my personal library was well-stocked with books I hadn't actually got around to reading. Still, I did have some that I knew would be of use. For example, I had previously bought three titles about building birdhouse from a sale at Norli bookstore in the early eighties, years before I had even thought of writing a novel about it. Life is full of strange coincidences.

The question was whether I should read all the books at once or pick one that seemed to inspire the most confidence. The question was soon answered after a quick perusal as two of the books seemed to have been thrown together just to make money. They were full of very little concrete information that I needed. The wrong materials to choose; environmentally unfriendly solutions. No, I quickly discovered which was the best book, no doubt about it.

With the book in my hand, I crept under the duvet and began to flick through it. Instantly, a new world opened up before my eyes with goals and material choices to be made, bird species, the sizes of birds and a mass of references to life in the forest and a mode of living that was completely alien to me. It was fascinating, but to be honest I didn't understand a word of it. What was the difference between a sparrow and a great tit? God only knows!

I remained in bed for a while, trying to get to grips with the book. But no matter how hard I tried, I just didn't get it. And that meant trouble. It also had considerable ramifications as far as my novel was concerned. Without the birdhouses, the narrative would be utter drivel. It would be all over the place, too dreamy. I needed the story about the birdhouses to anchor the project in the real world, yet simultaneously keep the dream alive!

I pulled the duvet over my head. I was tired and dejected. During the course of a couple of days I had lost both my favourite socks and my collection of a-ha records, as well as a whole host of other more or less valuable items. But had I done anything about it? Had I, for example, contacted the police about the graveness of the situation? Had I made use of my contacts for anything other than being flattered or rebuked or eliciting rancid comments about the state of modern literature? The answer to these questions was rather depressing. I lay a long time in the dark sighing heavily.

Then suddenly three likely lads jumped out of the ceiling and reached out their hands to me. It was Pål, Morten and Magne.

"Don't give up," said Morten.

"Carry on with what you're doing" said Magne.

"Move to London!" urged Pål.

What lads! I thought, now inspired. So strong! So independent! What iron will! They ventured out into the world, not giving a fuck about staying in the little safe haven that is Norway; Norway, with all its small-mindedness and backstabbers. Pål, Morten and Magne were upstanding members of the community too. They didn't drink. They didn't swear. They didn't harass old ladies. In other words, I told myself, they didn't spend their time fannying about, wasting their time with irrelevant things.

I hauled the duvet to the side and got out of bed, sensing the lightness of my body again. It was as if I had cut loose and was standing in front of the great, gaping whirl of freedom. The wind of freedom gusted from great heights, giving my dreams new impetus.

I didn't answer the phone when it rang. I let my answering machine pick up. Helle's longwinded school teacher's voice filled the room. She reminded me about dinner with her parents that evening. *"It will be just the four of us."*

She still hadn't got it into her thick skull that I had no intention of participating in the dinner she was talking about! I really could not stand women who collected old flames like they were teddy bears.

US FOUR! What on earth did she mean? Four with me, or four with her new beau? Did she think that I was such a hungry, lonely wolf that she had to take care of me like she ran some kind of soup kitchen for the homeless and down and outs? There was no way I was going to tag along as odd man out.

I picked up the receiver and dialled her number. It rang once and then twice before I hung up. Perhaps this was too serious a topic to talk about over the phone? This surely needed to be said face to face, clearly and succinctly along with the necessary paralinguistic information conveyed by the waving of arms. If she couldn't understand my softly softly approach, I'd have to show her the full force of my intentions.

I hesitated for a moment. Didn't I have an important errand that evening? I had to go and see Higgins to clarify the questions I had about building a birdhouse.

I decided I could pop in to Helle's en route to Higgins and clarify the situation. But what should I wear? I glanced into my wardrobe. There were fifteen black suits hanging neatly in a row. None of them were mine.

Helle's father stood mixing a cocktail. He had lime and juice and vodka and everything he needed. He was in a splendid mood. If it wasn't enough that he was about to become a grandfather, he was also en route to Spain with his wife.

"What do you say about a little Spanish something before we eat, Hobo?" he said.

I glanced over at the dining-table. Yes, there were four places set. I didn't doubt that. But had the baby's father shown up yet? No. It looked like things were going to get extremely embarrassing for the hostess and her parents. It was embarrassing for me too. I hadn't expected the guests to be there when I arrived.

"No thanks," I said.

"No?" said Helle's mother. "You can have a drink even if Helle isn't going to."

"Of course," I said.

Helle came in from the kitchen. The smell of Boeuf Bourguignon wafted after her and I realised that I hadn't eaten for a while. I needed to get going soon so I could find the nearest hot dog stand.

"Can you open the wine, Hobo?" said Helle.

The wine, yes! When it came to that sort of thing I was a pro. So I duly took it upon myself to take care of that duty before I left, if not for Helle's sake, then to show my sincere gratitude to her parents. I went into the kitchen and found a corkscrew which looked a lot like one I had once bought by postal order when I was a teenager. But no matter. With a firm YANK of my wrist, the job was taken care of.

It was now just a case of getting Helle on her own for a moment so I could speak seriously to her before I took my leave of her and her family for good. The sight of her father standing there mixing his drink reminded me of all the drinks I had previously drunk with these people. Every single drink appeared before my eyes: White Lady, Tom Collins, Cuba Libre.... This had nothing to do with sentimentality on my part. I was merely hungry and thirsty and three drinks were standing ready on the table. Plus, the final guest had not shown up.

"There you go," Helle's father said.

"Should I really?" I said.

"You've never said no before," said Helle's father.

"Good lord," I said, "I don't say yes to any old thing, you know!"

"Take whichever drink you want," Helle's father said. "They're all really strong!"

Helle's parents were, for the most part, very pleasant people. A bit annoying, perhaps, going on and on about their imminent trip to Spain, whilst Helle rummaged around in the kitchen. Both of them were recently retired and now they wanted to get away to their house on the Costa del Sol and sort out a few repairs on the house before the autumn storms kicked in for real in the old country.

"Work is like pouring petrol on the spirit's fire, as Lorca says," I said.

"Did you say Mallorca?" Helle's mother asked.

"He said Lorca," Helle's father said.

"Do we know him?" she said.

"Not that I know of," he said.

"We mostly hang out with other Norwegians," explained Helle's mother.

"Apart from craftsmen though," said Helle's father.

"Is *Lorca* a craftsman?" Helle's mother said.

"Lorca is Spain's greatest ever poet!" called Helle from the kitchen.

"Spanish craftsmen aren't any better than Norwegians, but they're cheaper," Helle's father said.

The alcohol went to my head first. That's normal. From there it continued through the rest of my body like warm water from an oil burner that's turned on again in the autumn. A calm atmosphere descended upon Helle's living-room. It was about time I made a move and left!

"Thanks for the drink," I said, and put my glass down on the table.

"You're welcome," Helle's father said. "I hope you don't mind that I took the opportunity to try out your mixer?"

I hadn't noticed this until now. It was just like all the other mixers I'd ever seen, but now I saw that there was something familiar about it.

"I'm off now," I said to Helle who was in the kitchen.

"Can you ask them to sit down at the table?" said Helle.

"YOU CAN SIT DOWN AT THE TABLE NOW!" I bellowed into the living-room.

Helle turned around and gave me a serving dish.

"Put this on the table," she said.

The odour of rubbish hung in the air around the entrance to Higgins' place. If it had been Grønmo, I would have looked about to see if there were seagulls. Higgin's boiler suit lay in a bundle outside and when he eventually opened the door, he stood there in his underpants. And we're not talking about a cool pair of baggy boxershorts; we're talking super tight 1970s Y-fronts!

"Am I disturbing you?" I said.

"Yupp," said Higgins.

Higgins shoved a hand down his pants and straightened his tackle. He bent his knee to get a better angle, and as he drew his hand back he made a point of pulling up his pants a couple of centimetres over his bulging belly.

"I need help building a birdhouse," I said.

"Well, you've come to the right man," said Higgins, and he turned and went back into his studio.

"Birdhouses are best made with 12-15 cm wide un-planed planks of wood, explained Higgins. "Use the same plank for the walls, roof and bottom."

Higgins rummaged around the studio for a quarter of an hour. Each time he found something that might be of use, he dragged it through the room in my direction.

"What sort of bird is going to live in it?" asked Higgins.

"It's not important," I said.

"There's a big difference between sparrows and great-tits," he said.

"Really?" I said.

"You don't have a clue!" said Higgins.

Whilst Higgins sawed the materials, I sat on a cardboard box and digested the meal I had consumed at Helle's. I had never eaten so much or laughed so much! I had felt a certain responsibility to entertain them as I sat with the three of them, Helle and her parents, so I had made an effort. First of all, I had to do justice to the food. And it was also part of my job to make up for the fact that I was there as a stand in for Helle's new boyfriend. The mysterious Mr X who didn't have the manners to make an appearance. It was a really absurd situation, of course. When Helle's father suddenly clinked his glass with a spoon and stood up to hold a speech, things got even funnier. He spoke warmly about the institution of marriage, families and love. I laughed so much I almost fell off my chair.

"For pupils at primary school it's an advantage if the pieces are cut up," said Higgins. "Do you need me to cut up the pieces beforehand for you?"

"Yes, please," I said.

So we started. Higgins gave instructions and I did my best at the carpentry. Of course one or two nails went crooked and at least once I managed to hammer my thumb instead of the nailhead; however, I was so enthusiastic and zealous that it hardly bothered me.

"This is really fun," I said.

"Absolutely," said Higgins.

"You've made birdhouses before, haven't you?" I said.

"Never," said Higgins. "But we ought to stain it and line the roof. And the roof has to open so that the box can be checked during the nesting season."

Safe and sound back in my apartment, I put the birdhouse on the desk in front of me and looked at it. It was solid and well-made, with a hole at the front the size of a fully-grown thumb. I now knew much more about birdhouses and the lives of birds so I could carry on writing.

On the way home from Higgins I decided that I'd take a quote from the "Birdhouse Builder's Oath of Ethical Conduit" to use at the beginning of my novel. Before returning to my desk to write, I put on *Headlines and Deadlines* and waited for Morten Harket's falsetto to begin. As he started to sing; I put my pen to paper:

The Birdhouse Builder's Oath of Ethical Conduct:
  - *Don't put up more birdhouses than you can build.*
  - *Fasten the boxes so they don't blow away.*
  - *Don't disturb the birds whilst they are eating.*
  - *Don't eat the eggs and chicks.*
  - *Clean the box after you've used it.*

Now that the writing was underway, I realised that I ought to include a Thank You at the start of the book. It seemed appropriate. Up until fairly recently I would have dedicated the novel TO HELLE. Obviously I wasn't going to do that now. People would wonder what was going on if a book was published dedicated TO HELLE at the same time as she was having another man's child. I didn't want to add to the confusion anymore than necessary. Besides, rumours had probably spread across town ages ago and I was completely uninterested in having to explain things to journalists when the book was launched. How could I have any trustworthiness if I wrote TO HELLE in the book? I would have to vehemently deny that it was my child. Perhaps Helle was the kind of woman that appealed to and was attracted to a vast variety of different types of men. One had been extremely tall, I remembered from having seen one of her photo-albums. He was tall, but not dark-haired; oh, and he collected paper serviettes. He had several thousand of them. I gather it was one of the reasons their relationship came to an end. He was more concerned about his serviettes than her.

I had to acknowledge that the theme of children had been mentioned on a couple of occasions during my relationship with Helle. But had I been interested in discussing the matter further? Of course, I had heard the old biological clock ticking. I heard it ticking as I lay next to her in bed at night. It ticked when we went for a Sunday walk in the park and when we did the washing-up after eating dinner in front of the TV. I saw it in the look she had as she watched the prams in the park, her over-developed interest in the children's section at Hennes & Mauritz. But I had kept my mouth shut and looked in a different direction.

Having children was not really something a genius should take on board, I thought. Think of all the mess that accompanies children! All the to-ing and fro-ing, and arguing and all the PARENTS IN LAW who call up and bother you with meaningless questions like whether the infant has big enough wellington-boots. They would no doubt call just at the wrong moment when you were on the point of a major creative breakthrough. Something of real significance for humanity.

No, there wasn't room for children in my life. Absolutely not. Besides, it was morally wrong to bring children into a world where there are insufficient daycare places. I was a strong supporter of equal rights for both mothers and fathers in that both should have time away from the child. I did, after all, have some sympathy for women.

It must be very difficult to be married to a very gifted, talented man, I thought. How had it been to live with the great Leo Tolstoy, for example? Probably a nightmare. Mrs Tolstoy's lot was that she was a dynamic, talented, very together personality. And in contrast to most men, Tolstoy was extremely loyal; however, he had the sexual appetite of a rabbit and harassed his wife for his daily oats.

Mrs Tolstoy gave birth twelve times. And as soon as the new born arrived, Mr Tolstoy knocked her up again. Couldn't he have occupied himself a little longer? Perhaps made *Anna Karenina* a couple of chapters longer, for example? It didn't get any better though because in later years Tolstoy took it upon himself that he and his wife should live devoid of carnal pleasure. Did he manage it? Did he heck! Tolstoy was at it continually.

I recognised a figure as I passed the Western Cemetery. A man dressed in black stood between two trees playing a saxophone. People were on their way into the large chapel and up from the crematorium chimney climbed thick, viscious smoke. I turned off Sørkedalsveien and left my bike in the car park.

Haagen looked tired. His suit was crumpled and his shirt collar was all askew.

"I've forgotten what I was going to play," said Haagen.

" 'Öppna Landskap' by Ulf Lundell?" I ventured.

"No," said Haagen.

" 'Lys og varme'?" I said.

"Maybe," said Haagen. "Or was it 'Captain Black Bill'?"

I couldn't really help him here. He was on his own on this one. Just as we all are when it comes down to it. But at least I could always give him a mental pat on the back. It didn't cost anything.

"How's it going otherwise?" I asked.

"I want the key," said Haagen

"Who doesn't?" I said.

"I've been thinking about our trip," he said.

"The bus ride?" I said.

"It's been bothering me," he said.

"How on earth can Tårnåsen bother you?" I wondered.

"Nothing was going on there," he said.

So Haagen was letting himself get all bothered by a trip to

Tårnåsen? Good grief! Of all the things he could have chosen to worry about. Haemorrhoids. A frozen saxophone mouthpiece. And he chose to worry about Tårnåsen!

A man from the crematorium waved at us from the building.

" 'Öppna Landskap'," I said.

Suddenly, Haagen grabbed hold of me by the scruff of my collar, and shook me.

"It's bloody time you gave me a key!" he said.

No one opened when I rang Mrs Høilund's door. I couldn't see her through the front door, but I could see that in the kitchen there were five bottles of red wine ready for opening. I bent forward to see what they were. Luckily, it was some cheap crap from Southern Ukraine where the corks weren't very difficult to open. I knew this from experience.

Mrs Høilund was lying on the rug in the living room. I saw her through the living-room window between two cactus plants. What on earth was she doing down there? Holding her breath in the pursuit of eternal fame in the Guinness Book of Records? I didn't have a clue. Old ladies and cars are two things that remain a constant mystery to me.

I sat down on the steps and waited for a bit. I had a good view up over the hill and started keeping an eye out for Pål and Lauren. But all I could see were small sparrows or wrens hopping about. Pål and Lauren had no doubt headed back to New York ages ago. Back to the seething metropolis and the Manhattan Skyline.

After leaving Mrs Høilund's, I cycled to Vinderen, a small centre with a handful of shops, places to eat and a subway station. An ICA supermarket caught my eye as did a rather trendy furniture store called R.O.O.M., which I went into in the hope of finding a new sofa.

I must admit that some of the furniture didn't look so bad, but it was considerably more expensive than IKEA. And wasn't an uncomfortable sofa the worst enemy of genius, second only to children?

"Do you need any help?" asked a lady, addressing me in Swedish.

"A glass of water please," I said.

"Aren't you feeling well?" she said.

"No, but I've just completed making a new table at home." I said.

I told the shop assistant about my building blocks and the table that was made of classy poetry.

"I mostly read detective fiction," she told me.

"Detective fiction?" I said.

I looked more closely at this woman. She had that typically Swedish blonde hair that was probably the result of a good dose of bleach or some other chemical product. Or maybe it's a consequence of the pollution that affects Stockholm and the other major cities in our neighbouring country, I thought, bending forward trying to catch a glimpse of the colour of her roots. They were as light as angel hair. SO here was a lady who took care of her appearance.

"Within that genre, I prefer my own novel *The Letter*," I said, "which was once reported to the police."

"So you're a writer?" she said.

"Yes," I said.

It was her turn to look at me. And I liked the way she looked at me with a certain interest. She stood up straight, pushing her chest slightly forward. Yes, indeed! It probably wasn't particularly inspiring to hang around here all day with lifeless furniture. The appearance of a genuine writer stepping in over the threshold was probably really something!

I was just about to touch the breast that was closest to me when I realised that my throat was exceedingly dry. I signalled to the girl that our conversation was now over and left coughing all the way to the café next door.

"A glass of water, please," I said.

"Anything else?" the girl behind the counter said.

"Just that," I said. "And a cappuccino, please."

"Single or double?" asked the girl.

After I'd paid and sat down at a table, I realised that this was turning out to be rather an expensive trip. I couldn't just go out and about on the swank side of town, splashing money about on a whim. Or at least I'd have to do some more work for Herman to cover it. I stirred my coffee, glancing about the café.

It was clearly the meeting-place for all the mums in the area as well as the well-to-do ladies. There were numerous prams in the entrance way and there was plenty of lively conversation going on over cups of coffee and ciabattas. At the next table to mine there was even a man with a baby-buggy. Even though there was a sign above the counter requesting that patrons leave buggies and prams outside, the over-zealous father had naughtily brought his inside. He was sitting there writing a shopping list in a notebook.

Please refrain from breast-feeding in the furniture department out of consideration to those customers who are shopping, it said on a sign.

No problem there, I thought, with a glance at my neighbour. Strictly speaking it didn't apply to this chap either but I wasn't entirely sure of men who put their career on hold and went on paternity leave whilst their wife was unfaithful with colleagues at work.

The baby began to cry. The man turned around and picked the baby up out of the carriage. The baby stopped crying and seemed to want to be snuggled into his father's breast. It was way too intimate a sight for a public café as far as I was concerned!

The man carried on with his shopping list whilst the baby seemed content to suck on his father's sweater. Had I seen this man before? If he had had a beard he would have looked like one of Helle's colleagues.

Or was it possibly the man I had seen in the street a week before. The man who had topped the American hit parade with the song "Take On Me"?

I was stunned. It was Mr Waaktaar himself! This time in a sweater and with a baby! Here he was a bright autumnal morning, no doubt working on the lyrics to his come-back album.

It was quite amazing, really. Father and pop star in one. I was impressed that he was capable of simultaneously being so much. I had problems simply hoovering and paying the bills. Hell, even sleep wore me out. But there HE sat, nonchalantly writing the lyrics to a new hit with little Augie on his knee. It seemed as if something great and something mundane was being juxtaposed right before my eyes!

I stared at his hand as he wrote. It was impossible to see what he was writing from where I was sitting, but I sensed that the words flowed easily as, without hesitation, Waaktaar composed sweeping sentences as they occurred to him.

Even if it looked easy from a distance, I suspected it probably wasn't easy to write about all his misery. And then it occured to me, all at once, how striking the contradiction was between the lightness of Waaktaar's music and the contents in

many of his lyrics. Some of his lyrics sounded practically sui-
cidal, yet they were reduced to the kind of stuff you hummed
along to. As I looked at him, full of respect for him, I was struck
by how convivial Waaktaar appeared. He was a composer capable of capturing human weakness and wrapping it all up in
catchy, sing-along melody.

How often in life had I managed to dodge depression and
misery by suddenly losing myself in the pleasure of something silly? Like pop music or stupid jokes? Or silly game
shows with superannuated celebrities in the starring role?

After ten minutes Waaktaar put the child back down in
the pram and got up. It was clearly time to go. It was probably time to get back to his home studio to record a demo of
the new song he was working on. And the child? Did he get to
sleep? Or perhaps Waaktaar employed Augie on bass, having
taught him using the well-known method used by the Dis-
similis musicians – colour coded chords that make it easier to
play, easier to create music that gets inside your head?

I waited a few minutes before I got up and followed Waaktaar. He must have been in a rush because when I got outside
he was gone, nowhere to be seen. I smiled, recognising myself
in this. When something needed to be created, it had to be
created NOW!! Otherwise, why bother? I was well aware of the
intense pressure an artist feels sometimes. Clearly, there were
things that HAD to be expressed. If things are allowed to build
up for too long without being expressed, it can go really badly.
There have been too many examples of this throughout his-
tory. Some abuse alcohol or drugs; others beat their wives or
simply decide to cut off part of their body and send it in the
post to some poor unwitting soul.

I pushed the bike and looked around a bit. Waaktaar was
nowhere in sight. All I could see were young wives from the

well-to-do houses nearby out shopping. The back-seats of the cars had empty child-seats. The kids were no doubt at some Tom Murstad-kindergarten up the hill, in deep discussion with other kids. There was undoubtedly sound-proof sand around all the children's playgrounds here, and helmets and kneepads for every outdoor game.

I decided to buy some buns to eat on the way back to town so I headed towards the ICA supermarket on the corner and entered the premises at full speed. The supermarket was quite different to my local store, Herman's Corner, which wasn't just the place where I purchased my groceries but was also my current place of employment. This store, however, was much bigger and very impersonal. Luckily, I managed to seize the last bag of raisin buns before an obtrusive woman grabbed them.

Holding the bag close to my chest, I quickly made my way to the checkout.

On the way I managed to stumble into the diaper section. It was a world I knew little about. There were several brands and sizes and everything seemed too much for an inexperienced chap like myself.

A baby-buggy obscured my route to the checkout. Sensing a whiff of claustrophobia, I tried to squeeze past.

As I did this I glanced down at the pram. Wasn't that Augie, lying there looking back up at me with big eyes? He'd probably not seen anything like me before – a short bloke with curly hair.

It didn't seem to scare Augie at all though. He actually smiled at me so I lifted my hand and said "Hi" back. Pål was squatting down a bit further away rummaging amongst the packets of diapers.

I thought for a moment about going over and telling him

how much strength and inspiration his music gave me in my work. Shouldn't I show my gratefulness in some way or other?

The Poetry Express was standing outside Herman's when I cycled back. Higgins and Herman were standing there lifting a stack of flattened cardboard boxes into the truck. As they let go it fell with a thump, which reverberated throughout the vehicle.

"What on earth are you doing?" I wanted to know.

"We're furnishing," said Higgins.

"With cardboard?" I said.

"I got to try Herman's bale-presser," said Higgins.

"Congratulations," I said.

Borrowing Herman's bale-presser was a dream Higgins had borne for a long time. I was delighted that he had now achieved his dream.

It was then that I noticed that "Worstward Ho" was lying in the back of the vehicle and on the doors posters had been put up about the remaining show at the Four Hens. The image was a hand-coloured drawing of "Worstward Ho" with a border of saxophones and books around it.

Higgins explained enthusiastically that the paper bales were going to function as seats backstage at the back of the rubbish room as well as shelves for the travelling gallery. All that remained was to knock together the tiny stage which was to be assembled by lifting. Then *The Poetry Express* would be ready for the off.

"Whether it's to Tynset or Tryvann Stadium," said Higgins,

satisfied.

I was impressed and lost for words. However, given that I maintained a certain distance to the project, I merely patted Higgins on the back and smiled.

Herman, for some reason or another, wasn't as happy as Higgins about things. Perhaps Higgins had mucked up the bale-press, or perhaps the day's takings in the store had dramatically decreased during the course of the day.

"Is anything wrong?" I said.

"You've been gone four hours," said Herman.

Me? All I'd done was have a look around the houses on the west of the city! I'd had a cup of coffee and then gone to a shop. Time flew by like a sparrow caught in a headwind.

"I thought you were dead," said Herman.

"Dead?" I said.

Death, if the truth be told, was not something I really considered very much. Even if it was something I would probably experience one day, it was far too soon to be thinking about things like that.

"Where have you been?" asked Herman.

"You know full well where I've been," I said. "I've been to your aunt's, weighed down by cabbage and tonic water."

"No delivery boy has ever stayed longer than absolutely necessary at aunt Hulda's," said Herman.

What did he know about what was necessary, I wondered. Besides, I didn't like his tone. Did he think he had the right to know everything about me just because I sold him a bit of my excess capacity to work? If that was the case, it was a very poor exchange. And I had no intention of telling him about my private meetings with Pål Waaktaar or any other celebrities who might feature in my private life. Besides, there wasn't really much to say. The bird had flown from the bush, so to speak, before I managed to get it in my hand.

Herman was just worried about aunt Hulda as it turned out. The reason for this was that she hadn't answered the phone.

"How did she seem when you were there?" asked Herman.

"Hmm, a bit passive, perhaps," I said.

"What do you mean by that?" asked Herman.

"Forget the bit about passive," I said. "Irritated is a better word."

"She's usually pretty happy when she gets her bottles of wine opened," said Herman.

"I also thought about that," I said. "But she didn't want to open the door when I knocked."

"Really?" said Herman.

"When I looked in through the living-room window I saw her on the floor," I said. "It looked like she was trying to hide. It was like she wanted me to think she wasn't at home. I put the things on the doorstep and left."

Herman furrowed his brow, and looked concerned, then told me that his aunt Hulda always answered the telephone, although there had often been other problems.

"She can be very stubborn at times," said Herman.

"That's incredibly childish," I said.

"One year I didn't even get a Christmas present from her," said Herman.

"Goodness me, that's just not on," I said.

"We sat there all Christmas looking at each other without saying a single word," said Herman.

"And you call her your aunt?" I said.

"She's good at heart," said Herman.

I met Helle on my way back to the apartment. She was standing outside Hult & Hansén, the estate agents, looking in the window. If she hadn't seen me I would have sneaked past. If you want to get on in the world, you don't have time for small talk on every street corner.

"How about a cup of coffee at the Four Hens?" she said.

She had a free period and didn't have anything better to do than guzzle coffee.

"I think it's a ridiculous habit you Norwegians have to drink coffee all the time," I said.

"You Norwegians?" said Helle.

"Yes," I said.

"You're just as much a Norwegian as I am," said Helle.

"I belong to the world," I said.

I regretted it the moment I sat down at the regulars' table at the Four Hens. I'd really decided to go along with Helle's suggestion of coffee, just to see how long she was prepared to carry on playing this game of hers. I was more than ready to tell her one or two home-truths, and wag my finger at her. But then it was nauseating to sit there and listen to hollow words about being friends. It was repulsive.

I hadn't been to the Four Hens since the incident with Hagbart and whilst Helle went over to Hjort to buy coffee for us, I glanced around the floor looking for any remaining drops of blood. There wasn't much to see. Maybe a drop of blood from a nosebleed or something, no larger than a fifty-øre piece. I felt as if I had been duped.

No, damn it, I said to myself. I was a creative being who needed a bit of peace and quiet from time to time! Had I sacrificed work on my novel, my study of the art of building bird-houses, taken time off from MY GREAT NOVEL, just to listen to what my ex-girlfriend had got to say?

"Do I have to drink the whole cup?" I said. "I won't manage my dinner if I do."

"Watch the pennies and the pounds take care of themselves!" said Helle.

Hmm, so she was in the mood for frivolous social intercourse? As if there was something humorous about the situation? Hadn't she thought, for example, about all the dangers that are associated with having a child at her age? The child, for example, might have a harelip. It wasn't a joke. And you couldn't just do what poor Inger did in Knut Hamsun's *Growth of the Soil* and abandon the child in the forest because it wasn't exactly what had been ordered. Punishment came sooner or later. Mr Hamsun had demonstrated as such in a striking way.

I thought about the Hubbing case. There hadn't been anything in the papers about the child having a harelip. A child had been found amongst the leaves. Who had buried the dead child there?

I drank a bit of my coffee. I had to get cracking if there was any hope of me finishing it before Hjort started switching the lights off.

"Don't you love me anymore?" asked Helle.

"LOVE ME ANY MORE?" Ha! Ha! Talk about turning something on its head. I looked over my cup at her. What kind of game was she playing? I had to be on the lookout, play with a poker face and keep my cards close to my chest. Either that or I'd be in serious trouble.

"Does it matter anyway?" I said.

"What do you think?" said Helle and patted her stomach.

I had been involved with cynical women before but this really took the biscuit. Was she trying to sort out some kind of back-up if all the other potential fathers let her down?

As if I could be the father to the little seed that was growing inside her as she sat there? Me, who could hardly remember the last time we'd even slept together. Had we even had sex in the last five or six years?

"I've been fired," I said.

"I heard," said Helle.

"Really?" I said.

"They told me when I tried ringing you at the paper," said Helle.

They probably did, the bloody telltales! It wasn't a surprise that the papers were full of gossip, but they could bloody well keep their mouths shut instead of giving out personal information to complete strangers.

"The kitchen going be nice?" I asked.

"Won't it?" said Helle, brightening.

"Don't ask me," I said.

Helle looked at me despairingly and took a sip of her coffee. I regretted the tone I'd used.

"How's it going?" I asked, with plenty of feeling in my voice. I spoke as if asking a child who has tripped and banged its knee and you don't have any plasters to help them with.

Helle shook her head and stood up.

"I have to get back to school," she said.

"What happened?" said Hjort.

He'd come over to clear the table and to get the latest gossip while it was still twitching.

"No idea," I said.

"Women are completely impossible to understand sometimes," said Hjort.

"Yes, aren't they?" I said.

"We do our best but is it ever good enough?" said Hjort.

"No," I said.

"No," said Hjort.

It felt fantastic to be understood for once. It felt so good that I moved over to the bar and ordered a Monrovian beer to show just how grateful I was. Hjort served it in the traditional way with a straw and a bowl of small dry biscuits. And just to top it off, he put on an a-ha song that was created for moments like this: "Touchy".

"Oh I'm TOUCHY, TOUCHY I am!" bellowed Hjort from the kitchen and then stuck his head out round the door and winked at me.

"Was the beer okay?"

"The biscuits were better," I said.

I remained seated and sucked a little on the straw, listening to the music. Touchy? There it was again, that tactile thing about a-ha! But this time everything was sort of turned on its head. Here you've been invited by the songwriter to TAKE

HOLD of him for a longer period and then it turns out that it's not so easy. He is overly sensitive and touchy. Now we get to hear about the pain of actually being touched. Touch can mean so many things, I thought. Sometimes its scratches and stings; it can be like a weeping sore to let people in close to you.

Thinking about Helle hurt. Perhaps I had judged her too harshly? She'd really messed things up for herself, the poor thing. Alone with a child and an uncertain future ahead. She probably didn't even know who the father was. Seeking and unsure, she'd probably mistaken sex for love, taken a grope in the dark as a substitute for real warmth and security.

I told myself I could surely be a bit more understanding about things. Even though I had right on my side, I didn't need to ram it down people's throats the whole time. Especially the throat of a woman in need.

"Another beer?" asked Hjort.

He had reappeared to clear away the empty bottle and try and squeeze the last drop out of the lemon.

"No thanks," I said, and took my leave. My gratitude didn't last forever and, besides, I had more important things to do. I was going to go completely against my principles and compromise: I was going to try and do something nice for Helle.

I stood still outside on the pavement thinking for a moment. What should I do? Buy flowers? That often cheered women up, or so I had heard. Especially red roses. They were both romantic and amenable. Trouble was, roses could give the wrong the signal, something completely outside my intention. I basically wanted to show Helle that I respected her. I had often read that the type, colour and number of flowers had a certain connotation and the last thing I wanted to do was get entangled in the complex web of love.

No, I decided it would be better to find something more palatable, I thought, and set off for the bookstore. Helle needed something that could help her through her difficult pregnancy and what better gift could one give but the gift of words.

"What did you say?" said the shop-assistant and glanced up from the paperback she'd been hiding under the counter. I couldn't see what it was, but from its size I suspected it could well be Huber Humpelfinger's *Erogenous Zones in the Middle Ages*, a book that seemed to be everywhere I went at the moment.

"The Norwegian Dictionary," I said.

She disappeared and I remained waiting, asking myself if it was possible to get through life without compromising. Great men aren't exactly known for compromising here, there and everywhere. It's usually a case of: "either you're with me or against me". Black or white. There are exceptions, mind. A really good example is what a-ha experienced during production of the track "The Blue Sky" from *Hunting High and Low*. In the lyrics Pål Waaktaar describes a young protagonist (guess who?) who is sitting in a café and feeling a bit dejected (as is usually the case in Waaktaar's world). Young and confused, he's standing face to face with life and all its difficulties and mysteries. There's a rather peculiar line that really catches your attention: "I'm dying to be different in a coffee shop."

A wish to be different? A wish to really stand out? To be someone else? Is he really talking about a young girl's attention? Or are we really talking about a desire to really stand out from the crowd? A desire to be seen? By The Other? By her? By him? By his father? By his mother? He almost pisses himself because of this need to be seen. In a café. Be different. To stand out so you're seen by the OTHER.

It was interesting to think that this very line had been changed during recording in London. Originally Morten sang: "I'm dying for a cigarette in a coffee shop." This could have brought the first-person narrator into contact with his surroundings in as much as he could have tried to cadge a cigarette from someone at a nearby table (something he probably would not have dared to do because of bashfulness and youthful insecurity). The producer wanted the cigarette cut. He was a bloody coward, piss-scared of stepping on the toes of militant anti-smokers in America. That's how the word "different" was switched into the line, giving the song another dimension of isolation. Rightly so, the first-person narrator wants to be seen, and in that respect keeps to his surroundings. He also wants to be different to the person that he is, or perhaps seen for what he is or even loved. The very thought made me shiver.

The woman returned with three books. They were published in 1918 and 1920, as well as a recent edition with a dirt-resistant plastic cover and several blank pages at the back of the book for your own notes. Here Helle could note down new words that she stumbled across, I thought, and cast a sceptical glance at the shop-assistant.

I didn't really trust her. She looked as if she was about to make a run for it with the books so she could keep them for herself.

I quickly checked the X-section in both books and noted that both *Xantippe* (a shrew, as well as the name of Socrates' wife) and *xeroform* (a salt that was used as an antiseptic) were both included. I could tell the dog by his coat.

"It looks okay," I said.

"Do you want it wrapped?" she said.

"One moment," I said. "You don't have a pocket edition, do

you?"

She looked questioningly at me.

"We have to remember that books like this will also be used by pregnant women," I said. "What do you think it's like carrying a brick like this around when you're heavily pregnant?"

The woman had clearly not considered this at all, no. She apologetically shook her head.

"We only have these," she said.

"Wrap it up then," I said.

Helle was standing talking with the same young man as before outside the classroom at one end of the corridor. I got the same queasy feeling in my stomach again as if I'd eaten something that had gone off. The two of them talked, deep in intense conversation. Before they parted Helle reached out and gently touched the boy on the arm. Then she disappeared into the classroom to share her heresy about Olaf Bull's life and poetry to even more innocent people. Seeing her touch him knocked me off balance. I had heard about the desirability of pregnant women and their effect on men, but what I had just witnessed was intensely perverted. On a par with abandoning a newly born baby in the forest.

It wouldn't surprise me if the whippersnapper was indeed the real father of Helle's baby. Yet at the same time he was just like a fly circling the honey. Of course, the honey would lose its sweetness once the baby was born. Helle would then realise that men, young and old, would have better things to do than serve her. She could end up being all alone.

The boy walked towards me.

"Are you looking for Helle?" he said as he approached me.

"How come?" I said.

"She's got English, now," he said.

The boy stopped and smiled at me.

"Hi Hobo," he said.

"Hello there," I said.

It was better to play friendly initially. If I was going to give him a good seeing to, it would have to be now. But I would have to get him outside and preferably down to the lake at Slottsparken first. Then I could whack him with the dictionary and fling him out into the water. I'd be doing both myself and humanity a favour. Of course, it would mean there would be no chance of making up with Helle and my present would have been wasted. Still, I could no doubt enjoy finding a use for it myself.

"Doesn't it get hot wearing a wooly beanie all year round?" I asked.

"Not at all," said the boy.

"When I was young we only used hats in the months that had an 'r' in," I said.

"Really?" said the boy, grinning at me.

There was something familiar about him. I recognised his smile from somewhere. It was then that it struck me. It was Harald, Helle's nephew!

"September and April were optional, of course," I said.

"Sure, I understand," said Harald.

"Put these on the shelves whilst I'm out," said Herman, pointing to a pile of plastic packets that were on the floor.

"What are they?" I wondered.

"Diapers," said Herman.

Diapers! I saw at once now! All kinds of diapers in different sizes. Just like Pål Waaktaar had bought at ICA in Vinderen. No wonder it took a bit of time. There were more choices here than towns in Belgium. For starters, there were lots of different brands and each brand had a stack of different varieties to choose from: for boys, girls, unisex! For those that weren't sure.

"It wasn't like that when I was a kid," I said. "We used terry cloth diapers."

"I doubt that," said Herman. He looked out the window. Higgins was going to give him a lift to his aunt Hulda to see how she was doing. I was going to mind the store whilst he was away.

"It's a fact," I said. "The whole of Drammen used terry cloth diapers before 1960."

"The disposable diaper was launched in 1955," Herman informed me.

"How come boys and girls need different diapers, then?" I said.

"They claim it's because boys and girls have a different shape," said Herman.

"Does it work?" I asked.

"It does work," Herman said.

Herman had changed from a store overall to a Burberry-coat from the middle of the 1950s. All that remained was a brief instruction on how to check the temperature on the fridge and frozen counters before he could leave and stay away as long as he liked. I was going to mind the store like it was my own novel.

"There are a couple of rules of thumb that we use in this branch of business," said Herman once we were behind the frozen counter. "Put your hand inside the freezer counter."

I did as he said.

"Do you feel anything?" he asked.

"It's cold," I said.

"How cold?" asked Herman.

"Very, very cold," I said.

"That's just how it should be."

Next it was the turn of the cold-counter.

"What do you feel now?" asked Herman.

"It's cool," I said.

"How cool?" asked Herman.

"Quite cool," I said.

"Be more precise," said Herman.

"It's like an autumn evening in September when you've been sitting on a stone and watched the sun go down on the horizon and the dark and cold comes creeping up from the ground," I said.

Herman returned after closing time looking rather sad. He had some bad news. He had found aunt Hulda dead with a bottle of red wine in her hand and a mouthful of cabbage. In the background French radio was blasting out.

"I've no idea how long that had been blasting out," said Herman. "But you can be sure that I switched it off instantly."

I suggested a spontaneous memorial on the spot with beer and cabbage which we ate with a bit of mayonnaise in memory of Herman's now deceased aunt.

For the most part Herman remained quiet, except for a couple of anecdotes about his aunt from the second world war. They were about as exotic as reports from anthropologists working with the indigenous population of Java. He then told me about the time he got new laces in his scout shoes, and it wasn't his birthday or anything. I sat listening with interest.

A solitary light was on in Helle's apartment but she didn't open when I rang on the outer door. I had a present to deliver before that also disappeared into thin air.

What did a pregnant woman all on her own do at this time of the day? She probably wasn't alone. Maybe her lover had shown up and taken her to the theatre or cinema in recompense for not turning up to the meet-the-parents-dinner. I decided the whole thing smelt of a guilty conscience.

I stood and waited a bit down on the pavement. A neighbour soon appeared on his way out and he let me in with a nod of his head. He greeted me as if he knew me from some place or other, probably recognising my face from the publicity photos for *The Letter* which my publisher had taken care of. I look pretty good in them even if I say so myself.

The present didn't fit through Helle's mailbox. The letterbox on her door was even worse. I might have managed if I could have ripped the book in half, say, at the letter K, for example, KABYLE (meaning a member of a Berber people inhabiting northern Algeria or the dialect of this people).

I rang the bell again but without result. I stood there, looking at the name plate on the door. It was a new brass plate which said: HELLE & HOBO LIVE HERE.

I certainly knew who Helle was; but there was no way I could claim I KNEW her. The last few weeks had clearly made that evident.

What should I do now? There I stood with a present in my hand and no one to give it to. I wasn't going to risk hanging it on the door handle. How often had Herman told me how the old dears stole like magpies here in Frogner? To hang the dictionary on he door would be like asking a pick-pocket to look after a wallet for a few moments.

I took my key ring out and shoved one of the keys into the lock. Amazingly it opened the door at once and soon I was standing in the darkened entrance of Helle's flat.

It smelt of something. Paint? I took a couple of steps forward and sniffed the air. Hardly. It was more like newly baked bread. I walked a few steps further before falling over some boxes that were stacked up alongside the wall. It wasn't as easy to hand over the present as I'd thought! I kicked the boxes and a couple of books fell out onto the floor. It was then that I saw the boxes contained copies of my first novel, *The Letter*. So: it was Helle who'd got her claws into them.

The bedroom door was open so I went over and peered in. I jumped when I saw Helle lying in bed. I was sure she was out! For a moment I thought I also saw a bundle next to her. A snoring manly bundle, stretched out on the bed. But upon closer scrutiny I realised it was just the spare duvet, scrunched up. The hope of a good night's sleep diminished with each new day of pregnancy, I supposed.

I am not a particularly curious man who goes out of his way to see what cards other people have been dealt; but I have to admit that I wanted to see how Helle had done with those crap paint-brushes she'd bought.

It was a shocking sight that met my gaze. She hadn't made a single decent brushstroke on the wall and the kitchen cupboards looked dreadful! It was worse than an insalubrious London backyard, I thought. She hadn't made any progress since I was last there and one-armed into dinner with her mother and father. The paint tray was on a newspaper on the floor and the brushes were lying on the draining board next to the sink.

It irritated me. I couldn't stand there and look at this mess. I stormed into the bedroom, ready to give Helle a piece of my mind about the tardy state of things.

I stopped in front of the bed. Was it sensible to wake her? To begin with, she probably needed a good night's sleep. What's more, I realised that my socks were rather sweaty and in need of changing. And as I hadn't thought about leaving the place without a clean pair of socks on, I opened Helle's wardrobe and peered in. There were piles and piles of clothes inside. I took hold of some rather sexy underwear and felt it between my fingers. What did pregnant women do with that kind of lingerie? It was soft and shiny like the skin of a fish. I placed it against my face and sniffed. It smelt clean and lovely, I had to admit. But then again anyone could manage that with a bit of WASHING POWDER and a good mood, I supposed.

Hold on a second! Wasn't that my smoking jacket hanging there in the wardrobe? I took hold of the jacket and checked the label. It was! Hanging here and used by another man! I shook with rage and began to check the rest of the stuff in there. A few moments later I had discovered that both the shirts and underpants were also mine.

I sat down on the bed and took my socks off. On Helle's bedside table there was a book about the different stages of pregnancy and I lay the dictionary down on top of it. If she didn't take a hint about what was good for her, it wasn't my fault.

Sleep collected me like a forgotten parcel now fetched by its owner, carrying me from room to room, and I dreamt dream after dream involving strange people and events: the woman in the sweetshop of my childhood, a reviewer from one of the larger Oslo newspapers or a talking moose from Thorbjørn Egner's well-known play.

I dreamt that it was raining. A violent rain that washed the streets clean. I didn't have an umbrella or a raincoat and I was walking and all the taxis had disappeared just like everyone else. After a while I arrived at the hospital and went looking for the maternity ward. It was as if everyone was waiting for me. They smiled at me. It made me a bit nervous and I went into the bathroom and looked at myself in the mirror. My hair was grey.

Helle wasn't in her room when I found it. The duvet lay thrown to one side and her slippers were gone from under the bed. A midwife came walking into the room with a baby.

"Time for a bit of food," she said.

"Perhaps you'd like to change him first," she said.

"You can do it in there," she said, and wheeled the trolly into the side room and then disappeared.

I looked about. There were towels and diapers and cloth and blankets. Everything that you needed. And the diapers were of the very best sort. I saw that at once. I looked at the tiny baby. He was the spitting image of Pål Waaktaar.

Helle brought in a tray with breakfast.

"Thanks for last night," she said.

"Yes, I put that on your bedside-table and fell asleep before I looked at a word of it," I said.

"You scoundrel!" said Helle, and ruffled my hair.

This was perhaps getting a bit intimate! I moved a little towards the edge of the bed.

"Have you read the book already?" I asked.

"No, I haven't," said Helle. "We can snuggle down with it

during the long autumnal nights!"

Yes, she could share it with her knight in shining armour if that's what she wanted. Even if I wasn't exactly in favour of sexual freedom, I believed the words to be common knowledge.

"Is everything okay?" I asked, worried.

"Oh, yes," said Helle.

"You're holding your hands on your tummy," I said.

"Am I?" said Helle.

"Yes, you certainly are," I said.

"I'm just saying 'hello' to her," said Helle.

"Her?" I said.

"I think it's a girl;" said Helle.

A girl! Helle hardly knew the back from the front when it came to girls! Now that I had got used to the idea of Helle as a mother, it was a boy I saw her with. The fact that it could well be a girl took me aback. A son could be useful. Someone she could teach correct Norwegian grammar too; someone who could put some order into her bookshelves.

"Eat as much as you like," said Helle.

On the tray were plates of eggs and bacon and glasses of juice. She'd even managed to put a few bits of melon on as well. The bacon was cooked just right: nice and crispy as I liked it. And the egg didn't have a drop of slimy egg white either.

After Helle left for work I went into the kitchen and had a look around in the daylight. The paint job was far from finished. There were gaps between the walls and the ceiling and the skirting boards and the green paint was having difficulty covering the previous incumbent. What's more, the holes in the wall from screws and nails hadn't been filled with putty and sanded like they should.

Strictly speaking it was nothing to do with me. If Helle

wanted to live with walls like this, then it was up to her. But it so pained me to see this that I just couldn't leave well alone. I filled all the holes with putty, sanded them down and then finished painting the walls with the necessary precision from top to bottom. It was much better. Really good.

As I walked across the courtyard, I thought I heard a familiar tune floating out from one of the flats. It was "Move to Memphis" from *Memorial Beach*. Whoever was playing it had a hi-fi that really belted out a lot of noise. The bass riff thumped in the window frames as Waaktaar's guitar crunched like broken glass on concrete.

I rang the bell for quite a while before someone let me in. I had my smoking jacket clenched firmly under my arm and as the buzzer sounded, I pushed the door open and zipped past the mailboxes and down the corridor. The apartment door was also closed so I had to lift my arm and knock again.

The music was abruptly silenced and I could hear rustling behind the door. I must say it was pretty tiring stuff to get to your own writing desk. But I guess it was just one of the hassles of being your own boss.

The door opened ajar and there was Haagen peering out from behind the security latch.

"Who is it?" said Haagen.

"Open up!" I said.

"Who is it?" said Haagen.

"I need to work. Open the door."

He unfastened the chain and opened the door. I was bowled over at the sight of him in a new black suit with a violet silk shirt and he looked red and flustered compared to his normal pale complexion.

"Are you wearing that this evening?" said Haagen.

"I've found my smoking jacket," I said and put it on.

"Oh, no," said Haagen.

"The smoking jacket stays on," I said, sitting down at my desk.

It wasn't easy concentrating with Haagen there in the room. He paced around, humming old jazz songs whilst trying on each and every second-hand suit he owned. In the end I got up and put on *Headlines and Deadlines*, which had seen such heavy use lately that it glowed like a waffle iron in its cover.

"Have you ever thought about moving to Memphis?" I asked.

"Where?" said Haagen, blushing.

"They've got good hamburgers there," I said.

Haagen disappeared out into the city, leaving the smell of aftershave and peanut butter. I finally got into the mood to write with the help of "Crying in the Rain" and was in the process of letting my protagonist build birdhouses. Now that I had had the chance to build my way through a whole birdhouse with Higgins' help, I could describe its construction and development in a really realistic, organic way: the selection of materials, the cutting out of the parts, and the boring of of the hole with the right diameter depending on what bird the was meant for, whether it was a sparrow, a great-tit or a wren, etc. The novel's protagonist spends the entire winter building birdhouses and when spring comes he climbs up trees to put them up. He finds one tree, climbs up and attaches the box securely. Thereafter it's a case of sitting down on the veranda and waiting.

What did the birds really want with birdhouses? They were a place to build a nest. A home for them and their family. Each birdhouse was a nest. Each nest was a home for a family of birds. Safe from the rain. Safe and sound from larger birds and squirrels with less than honourable intentions.

The hero sits on the veranda and waits.

Something monumental will happen soon.

Haagen and the band were almost finished rigging up the equipment when I got to the Four Hens. *The Poetry Express* stood parked outside and Higgins was heaving stuff about in his boiler-suit and sunglasses.

"Are you going to give us a hand or what?" he called out as I passed by.

That was fine by me. The balance between sitting still and physical activity was as crooked as the Leaning Tower of Pisa. I had been sitting on my arse writing and writing all day and I needed a bit of exercise. I'd nonetheless made significant progress, managing to finish writing before I came to a stand-still.

This was an old writer's trick that people like Homer used to play in the days of antiquity: they would suddenly just keep their mouths shut, indicating to their listeners they'd have to come back another day. Ten wild horses wouldn't get them to utter another word.

We manoeuvred "Worstwards Ho" out of the backstage area of *The Poetry Express* and soon it was lying on its back on the pavement, gazing at the stars. The word "back" of course was something I only said to myself. I accepted that modern art was open to interpretation and that my interpretation was no more correct than anyone else's.

"We'll put it in front of the door to the men's loos," said Higgins. "You're more open to something new if you're desperate for a piss."

I sat down in the bar and looked at a number of the texts that I had brought along with me, with a view to the coming reading. Hjort served me a lager without any head.

"You're learning," I said. "Thanks very much."

"It's on the house," said Hjort.

"Again?" I said. "You'll soon go bust if you carry on like that."

Haagen's band consisted of a saxophone, keyboard, bass and castanets. When Hagbart showed up with his bass, I was ready to leave but he came right over to me and apologised.

"I behaved like an idiot," said Hagbart.

"Me too," I said.

"No, I'm the one that was wrong," said Hagbart.

"If you insist," I said.

Of course, he was the idiot but the best approach is to always let people reason their way to this insight themselves. If it worked for Socrates, it worked for me.

Personally, I was mostly concerned about the geographical area around his eye, which looked like a map that had been coloured in with a set of colours consisting of blue, green and yellow and with a few flecks of red. But what could I do about it now? Done was done and he who dwells on the past gets nowhere in life, I thought.

Hagbart went over to join the rest of the band to tune his bass and soak his pigs trotters in water before the concert, whilst I looked through my papers again. I decided that I would read the most recent sonnet that I had written – the one I wrote in the police cell. It was both the right time and place to trip the light fantastic with classical poetry.

Haagen waved me over to the stage just as Helle showed

up in an attention-grabbing red dress which I recalled having bought for her on some occasion or other. She waved to me and I gestured with my glass, leaving her to interpret this as she wanted. I assumed she understood that I didn't want to take on the responsibility of a child that wasn't mine. I slept in her bed, OK? It could happen to anyone.

The plan, according to Haagen, was that the band would start by performing one song first and then I would recite a poem whilst they accompanied me. After that I would read a poem unaccompanied and then the band would play an instrumental. And on and on it went without me getting the logic behind it all.

"It's worse than doing the pools," I said.

"Take it easy," said Haagen. "I'll keep you up to date about what's happening as we go along."

The big question was whether I was going to sing or just recite one of my poems. I could also do a mixture of both where, for example, I sang the chorus or just sing-talked my way through it as I felt like it. We agreed that I would start off as if I was reading a poem but then sing if I felt like it.

"We'll find our way as we go along," said Haagen.

"To rubbish," I said.

A hullabaloo by the door interrupted me. It was Holm who had been stopped at the door with a bottle of vodka sticking out of his pocket. Seeing me, he called out something incomprehensible and took out a dog-eared journalist's notebook from his pocket.

"Let him in," I called.

The bouncer looked rather sceptically over at Hjort.

"Who is it?" said Hjort.

"The press!" I said.

An hour later it was completely packed in the bar. People were standing or seated everywhere and the bar itself had become a look-out point for the excited audience. An air of expectation hung over the place and by the table closest to the stage sat Higgins, Haagen, Hagbart and the others in the band, warming up, each with a beer. We'll have to get cracking soon, I thought, before the alcohol takes too strong a hold.

"You can't wear that," said Haagen, trying to pull off my smoking jacket.

"Give up," I said.

"You look like a dried up box of sandwiches," said Haagen.

"Thank you," I said.

"Give him your shirt, Higgins," said Haagen.

Higgins took off his Hawaiian shirt and I discretely changed tops behind Higgins' bulky frame.

"There you go," said Haagen. "A star is born."

For the first couple of seconds I was blinded by the lights. Then Haagen gave me a shove from behind and I stumbled out onto the stage and took hold of the microphone stand, hanging on for dear life.

It was quieter than the grave poor aunt Hulda would be lying in during the autumn. I stood, soaked in the light, sensing the faint odour of sweat and rubbish from Higgins' shirt, whilst one or two faces caught my attention amongst the audience. I saw Helle at a table with a bottle of mineral water in her hand; further back I could have sworn that Álvaro de Campos was straining his neck to get a better view of me. A couple of young girls at the front near the edge of the stage shrieked when I took hold of the microphone and said something inspiring about life, death, love and the universe. I looked out over the sea of people and sensed a warmth grow in me. Right at the back of the bar, leaning against the wall, stood Holm, staring at me with a saddened expression.

"I'll start by reading a sonnet," I said. "And like the great poet Håvard once said, a sonnet is not the latest model by Opel."

Waves of laughter engulfed me.

"A sonnet is a rhyming poem," I said.

"A-ha!!!" answered the audience.

"And this sonnet is about life here at the Four Hens," I said. And with that I read the sonnet: "On the Town".

He walked towards her, panting with desire.
"Is it you?", he said, and put down his guitar.
He smiled a lurid smile and lit a big cigar.
"Let's leave this place, together we'll be fire."

It enrages me that someone dumb and dire
Can try to pick up Helle in this bustling bar.
His pig-like hands won't get him very far,
When there's a better lover watching, full of ire.

But she was cold and sent him callously away.
And then he taunted her because his plan unfurled:
"It's your loss baby, if you will not play."
He cursed his luck in such a fickle world.
I saw his hands were heading Helle's thighs way.
So I smacked him hard for being bloody bold.

A couple of the girls at the front of the stage fainted during the reading. Then again, they might just have been lying down. But I didn't have time to dwell on this as there was an almighty sound that began first as a whisper and then turned into a roar, as the audience stood up. Applause and cheering filled the room and they demanded more.

"I love you," I said into the microphone. "I love you."

Helle smiled the sweetest smile and I almost bit my tongue off. Of course, she took everything I had said as deeply flattering.

I sat down at the table glowing, radiating light like a beacon. Helle bent down and gave me a hug and I let her do this, but as she went to kiss me in front of hundreds of curious fans I stopped her.

"It looked like you were born to be on stage," said Helle.

"Thanks," I said.

"And thanks for the poem," said Helle.

What was there to thank me for? I had written it for eternity, not to please her. Besides, I knew all about how women tried to wrap men round their little finger with a bit of flattery. Men are stupid but I'm the exception to the rule.

Haagen came over and gave me a pat on the back, and pulled me over to the bar.

"It went really well, Hobo!"

"Thanks, you guys were good too," I said.

"We want you to be involved on a permanent basis," said Haagen. "Higgins is the manager and we're going to travel the length and breadth of this country bringing poetry to the people."

"Can I take a pee first?" I said.

"Of course," Haagen said, generously.

I went into the toilet and sensed how my presence filled the tiny room, savouring every drop. Suddenly, I realised how Morten Harket must have felt when Magne and Pål urged him to move to London with them. Magne and Pål needed Morten to reach out with their music just as Haagen and Higgins now needed me.

The sound of a toilet flushing distracted me and then I saw Holm step out from a cubicle. He stared at me and then said: Ieeeet caaanj nexxxxs?

It is an understatement to say that I was inspired when I got back to the apartment from the Four Hens. I was really charged up and set upon making a final attempt to write my way through my novel in one last push. If I had to sit at my desk for forty-eight hours, keeping myself awake with stewed coffee and dry biscuits, I would. I decided I would have the first version ready before I stepped out amongst the chestnuts along Bygdøy Allé.

Perhaps I'd set my goals too low? Sure, the Nordic Council's Literary Prize was a good place to start but didn't my reception at the Four Hens demonstrate that I was made for bigger things? Wasn't the time right for me to dare to admit to myself that the Nobel Prize was within my reach – if I could just finish my work in peace and quiet?

A window in my apartment was open out towards the back courtyard. The stars looked down upon me between the walls of the buildings. I climbed in and walked towards my desk.

The first thing I noticed was that the birdhouse lay in the middle of a heap of dirty laundry on the floor. If Haagen thought I was going to do it for him, he was mistaken. There were stacks of reputable launderettes in this city, not that I could name any of them at that precise moment. But if I was forced to, I could rustle up a few addresses and telephone numbers.

It was then that I saw that my desk was gone! A black strip of dirt was the only witness that there had once stood an IKEA writing desk there. A desk I had come to be very fond of over the years. A desk that had witnessed many of my literary raptures on late autumn evenings.

It wasn't the end of the world, though, I thought. Desks can be replaced. Besides, a good author can create priceless literature just about anywhere and in any number of imaginable postures, I reminded myself. So I went over to the bed to retrieve my manuscript. I can't say I was surprised to find Haagen in the bed. I'd got used to one thing and another. I was used to struggling. And since Haagen was lying there, it was natural to see his saxophone lying in its owner's tranquil lap. It was more surprising, however, to see Hilde curled up in a corner.

I stuck my hand in underneath the mattress where I usually kept my manuscript.

Haagen grunted and turned over.

"Move your arse," I said, and stuck my hand further in.

I started pacing around the apartment. The very thought was almost unbearable. The brief seconds I was in its grip, it was as if the room called to me and my own misery, as if all my faults lay on the floor and not the dirty laundry of a shabby saxophonist by the name of Haagen.

I took a deep breath and stamped angrily on the floor.

"No!" I yelled.

I beat my hands against the wall.

"NO!" I yelled again.

The manuscript was gone.

This could not be happening to me. I had almost spotted land amidst the fog! I'd almost sensed solid ground beneath my feet! And now I was suddenly cast out on the open sea again without a map or compass.

As I've previously mentioned, the best way to control one's frustrations is by cleaning. And the most natural place to start is the drinks cabinet. I sat down on the floor in the kitchen and reached an arm into the cupboard under the kitchen bench. The first thing I detected was a drop of gin someone had left after a housing association get-together a few years earlier. The five of us had not even managed to finish off one bottle of gin! Having ascertained that the bottle was free of mould and its contents smelled as they should, I drained it in one gulp and lay the empty bottle in a bag from Herman's Corner.

Yes! It felt better immediately and I let my thoughts roam as I stuck my arm in the cupboard again.

What would Pål Waaktaar have done in my shoes? It was a very relevant question at this particular moment. Would he have given up and collapsed on the floor in a heap of tears? Would he have kicked and hammered the floor like a little child who has lost his pacifier?

Hardly. Pål was a man who stuck to his guns. He would probably have had a few doubts for a moment before lifting his head up and focussing on what was to come. Because there are a thousand things to grab hold of, aren't there? Weren't there other roads to Rome?

Actually, Pål had experienced something similar during his first time in London before Morten allowed himself to be persuaded to follow them over the North Sea to gamble everything on that which would become a-ha. When Pål and Magne came back after a break in Norway, they realised that their secret hiding place in the loft in the house they'd been staying in was no longer secret. They'd hidden their most precious stuff there so they wouldn't have to take it back home. The problem was that they had a couple of things to settle with the landlady from whom they had fled. You can guess she squealed with delight when she took the lid of the dustbin and emptied in the boys' precious things with a wicked grin.

Pål lost a whole collection of poems! In my arrogance, I had always doubted Magne and Pål's judgement on this point. What a ridiculous hiding place! I had wondered on numerous occasions whether they really were that stupid. But I understood the symbolic nature of this. So strong was their belief that they would return and be successful that they had left their most precious things to London and fate.

I put my arm in the cupboard again and took hold of another bottle. This time it was a whole bottle of coffee-liqueur. Coffee was just what was needed, I thought, and guzzled it down as if it was the last thing I was to do before going into battle.

I looked at the clock.

It was four-thirty AM.

Herman's bike was standing outside the backdoor of the store as usual with a crappy lock that I opened with the key to my notebook. Herman hadn't opened the shop yet but I saw him rummaging about through the window to the back store-room.

I placed the birdhouse on the front of the bike and rolled out onto the street. The sun was still low but the sky was blue. It was going to be hot today.

I thought about how grateful I was to Pål. He had given me so much without knowing it himself, but this was turning out to be a one-way relationship. You need to give something back, I told myself. You really need to give Pål a present.

But what should I give him? What do you give someone who has everything they need? I had a strong feeling that Pål wasn't the materialistic type. He was spiritual like me. And therefore the perfect present would be a copy of my book, *The Letter*, dedicated to him, I figured. Or maybe a birdhouse?

Weren't we talking here about a spiritual connection be-tween us? Twin souls, perhaps? Even if Pål hadn't realised it yet, he would now. If he gave it a bit of time. It couldn't be SO easy to sort the wheat from the chaff when you were as famous as he was. How many people wanted to pick a quarrel with a pop star of his ilk? And for what reason? He probably got people harassing him for money or sex. Or maybe they just wanted Waaktaar to light their way, be the shining star to their blacked out moon?

And what was it that made me think that there was something special between the two of us? many would ask.

It was just something that I knew, I would tell them.

My missing manuscript was just a confirmation that our lives were following the same path.

Waaktaar was undoubtedly a man with an acute appreciation of language and literature. He'd had a love of literature in his youth, losing himself in the worlds of Dostoevsky and Hamsun. Hadn't he run wild, lost on a literary high at the Waaktaar-family cottage at Nærsnes, a safe distance from the high-rise flats and terraced-housing of Manglerud, like a character in a Hamsun novel before the second London trip with a-ha, hadn't he?

Malicious tongues might suggest that the stories about Pål Waaktaar's literary interests were just a sham, part of building a-ha's image in the eighties. Personally, I didn't doubt for an instant the picture of the bookish pop musician from the less salubrious, east side of Oslo. Waaktaar undoubtedly read until his eyes hurt and his head ached whilst the other lads in the band worked to make money. The three of them dreamt of returning to London and Waaktaar's capital was HAMSUN. That's how it was. The best.

Sure, he flipped out and flapped around at the family cottage in Nærsnes whilst Magne Furuholmen was struggling as woodwork teacher and Morten Harket was working at a nursing home. What was real and what was imaginary wasn't easy to distinguish. Pan's flute sounded in the forest and romanticism and a belief in the power of nature blossomed.

The story about Pål Waaktaar and the moose, two kings who ran into each other out in the forest at Nærsnes, ought to convince any doubters about Waaktaar's genuine relationship to literature at that time:

One evening when Waaktaar was trotting out across the yard towards the woodshed – wearing white pants – something strange happened that truly propelled a-ha's career forward: a chance happening that underlined it was high time the boys headed back to London.

Waaktaar was lost in thought as he walked and stopped for a moment on his way to the woodshed and stared at the mounds of sycomore leaves that covered the ground at that time of year. He asked himself what these leaves were actually covering. The dead child from Hamsun's *Growth of the Soil*? The child who had a harelip like his mother and didn't have the right to life? Waaktaar took a couple of paces towards the piles of leaves and stared. No, he thought. It wasn't possible to make out any shapes in the leaves. And there was absolutely no question of his turning the leaves over with his foot! The mere thought repulsed him.

But just as he was going to go on to the woodshed, a moose rushed out of the undergrowth. Waaktaar spun around, certain that his white pants had antagonised the moose and that it was now going to attack him, and rushed back to the cottage where Magne stood in the doorway.

"Heavens above!" screamed Waaktaar "Help! The white pants!"

Did Augie recognise me? It wasn't impossible. There is something about me that makes a big impression on people. No, it wasn't the first time I'd experienced it! But children were different. They acted as if nothing was different or unusual for them, that they carried a wisdom that stretched back to when primitive man trudged around the planet, bare-footed and without a clue as to the idiotic things humanity would do in the years to come.

I bent down and looked more closely at the boy. No, this wisdom had a more recent air about it, I could see. Approximately the sixteenth century – renaissance, card games and brass musical instruments. He looked like a wise old man who had settled down after many years in service of the greater good. Just relax, little man, I thought, turning his toy around. If you're planning to stay awake, keep your mouth shut and don't start that screaming that cuts to the very marrow.

At that very instant he began to wail, making me jump. Everyone in the shop turned around and soon Waaktaar was there, picking his son up out of the pram.

"Do you know if they have Libero for 2-3 year-olds?," I asked Waaktaar.

The baby had already settled down. Waaktaar looked at me and answered.

"No idea. We use Pampers."

"Pampers?" I said.

"Yes," said Waaktaar.

"Pampers are certainly best," I said, "But I have a bit of a problem with my youngest daughter. She pees through Pampers diapers."

"Shit," said Waaktaar.

"It is pretty shitty," I said.

"Yeah, absolutely," said Waaktaar sympathetically.

"Up & Go work best," I said.

"Have you tried tightening the fastening tape a bit diagonally? It sometimes works with a bit of trial and error," said Waaktaar.

"Doesn't help," I said, shaking my head in defeat.

There was a moment's silence. I began hunting around in my pocket. If I was going to hand over my book, it had to be now. We had shared a moment of intimate conversation in the middle of a supermarket, a new father and a possible embryonic father-to-be. What was more natural than to surprise him with the book then and there? There was no doubt, after all, that this was a literary-minded man.

I searched my pockets. The book wasn't in my right pocket, nor was it in my left: I'd stuck it in my back pocket. But just as I located it and was about to hand it over, Waaktaar had disappeared. I saw him leave the store where Lauren was waiting for him outside. They were clearly in a rush because they began to babble just like an old married couple who haven't seen each other for three minutes. And with that they were gone, probably off to take the next flight to New York.

I was slightly jealous of Lauren. Pål had run out of the store as soon as he'd caught sight of her. If I had to outmanoeuvre Lauren to get Pål all to myself for a few seconds, I'd need a drink. So I went and got a six-pack, paid at the checkout and went outside.

Pål and Lauren were slowly strolling down the road. I actually didn't have the slightest thing against Lauren. But right at this moment she was a niggling fly in the ointment.

Wherever you may go, I'll follow.

I stood with the tips of my toes right on the boundary between public highway and private property. A few metres away was a magnificent house with a terrace at the front and a driveway and a solid-looking door behind which existed a completely different world. It was a world I had only read and dreamt about for so long, although I was certain I would be part of it one day.

A blue car was parked in the driveway and the baby-buggy was nearby. The car looked like an old Opel Sonette. To be honest, it was a bit of a disappointment. I expected Pål to have something a little grander – a sporty four-wheel drive or a classic Jaguar.

My stomach felt unsure. A man of my age could only take so much coffee liqueur. It was churning and a slight sense of nausea had appeared in the last few minutes. The only other thing I'd consumed was beer, just to keep myself hydrated. I'd been standing there for a long time: two hours and four minutes to be exact, half concealed by a bush. I had managed to misplace the bike on the way.

I wasn't feeling exactly on top of the world. It was like my body was trying to force me to my knees. But was this really anything to be concerned about? I was just going to give a present to a kindred-spirit. Nothing more, nothing less.

The message I'd written at the front of the book was simple and nice: 'To Pål from Hobo. Congratulations on being a father!'

The last part was an attempt to strike a chord with him. Children weren't exactly my area, but new fathers liked to be reminded of their status as family-providers whether they're successful entertainers or just tram drivers. All I had to do was knock on the door, introduce myself, and hand over the present. It wasn't much harder than that.

I downed another beer and went in through the gate. I was, perhaps, a little unsteady on my feet. Maybe my hair could do with a bit of a comb, but at least I was decked out in my smoking jacket and a Hawaiian shirt.

I put the empty bottle in the rubbish bin as I passed, but I wasn't one step further before I felt a pang of bad conscience. What kind of cheek was it to throw away your rubbish in someone else's bin without asking permission first? I returned to the bin and lifted up the lid again. The stench hit me as I bent forward. The bottle had fallen in between two ICA plastic bags stuffed full of rubbish. I felt a wave of intense nausea as I grabbed the bottle and slammed the lid shut.

It was then that I noticed my hands were covered in something red. Was there a dead foetus in the bin? The body of an old friend who had appeared at an inconvenient moment, just as the little one was going to bed? Yes, what really did lie hidden under "Sycamore Leaves"? I wondered. Dead bodies, raped and maimed children? Or just projected and repressed fantasies? I thought about the dark element in Waaktaar's lyrics. They were simultaneously superficial and deeply meaningful. The balance between success and failure. Had I really been so wrong about him?

The picture of my kindred-spirit suddenly grew a new dimension, but then I realised what the red actually was: pasta sauce!

I started to cry. Were we even more than kindred spirits? We liked the same food as well! The thought was immediately uplifting and I eagerly licked the sauce off my hand. Dolmio? Almost certainly, and after a quick rummage in the bin I found the empty jar which I shoved into my jacket pocket before continuing towards the front door.

Halfway along the driveway I slowed down. The sight of someone through a window sent me scurrying towards the garden instead.

It was better not to disturb them right then. The little lad was probably sleeping. I decided to take a look at the garden first instead.

The small family sat on the living-room floor. The parents were tickling and talking to the baby. His diaper had to be changed soon, from what I understood, as all the equipment was ready: a clean diaper, wet-wipes, a cream for sore bottoms.

I had a good view from where I was standing, able to see directly through the terrace door. But it surprised me that there was hardly any furniture at all in the spacious living-room. What was this then? Were these the kind of surroundings to bring up a child in? Or, I asked myself, is this how celebrities live? Without furniture but with a big bank account? Perhaps it's impractical to have so much standing about, gathering dust when you're out on tour?

The baby looked stupidly at his famous father and burped. It was all too much for me; I put my hand to my mouth and pressed my forehead against the pane of glass, and just as he removed the diaper from the little boy, nausea engulfed me and I threw up all over the terrace.

When I was finished I turned back to the door but saw that

176

they had gone. Sick was still dripping from the terrace as I went down the steps. I'd left the birdhouse behind. There was no one to be seen behind the curtains or out on the road, but in the distance I could hear the police sirens growing louder and louder.

"Highbrow?" said Hansson. "Can I give you a lift?"

She could always give me a lift, but WHERE TO was a completely different matter. I got in the back of the car and hoped for the best.

"Out doing a bit of research?" said Hansson.

"Out trying to clear my head," I said.

"Yes, us writers need that," said Hansson.

Yes, she'd said 'us writers' but I let it go. I was tired and needed to sleep.

"I was so inspired by our last conversation that I started a new poem," said Hansson.

"Good, Hansson," I said. "You're getting it together."

"It takes place in 2077," said Hansson.

"Really, why?" I asked.

"Dunno," said Hansson.

"Then you bloody well better find out!" I bellowed.

"I thought you said that you don't need to explain everything to the reader," said Hansson, a bit unsure now.

"You're right. The reader can damn well manage on their own," I said.

So Hansson began to tell me all about her poem, which she'd entitled *Sparrowlife* and had 23 different characters involved, and the catch was they were all related to each other in a surprising way.

I was soon sound asleep.

I woke up with a start and sat up in bed. Someone was running a bath and a dog on the floor above us was barking. What was standing over there? Wasn't it my writing desk? And on the desk lay a tidy pile of papers that I recognised.

The water in the bathroom was turned off and soon after that I heard the door click. I got up and went out to the kitchen.

Wow, it was really nice in there! The fridge, notice board and the Gauguin print were in place and the red kitchen cupboards created a lively impression against the green background.

On the table was a note:

Hello Hobo,
See you at the Four Hens at 12:00. Higgins is driving. Your suit's in the wardrobe.
Helle

An ice-cold cola was on the edge of the bath and it was then that I heard classical music coming from the living-room.

I could see her from where I was standing. She was moving between the dummies dressed in children's clothes in the shop next to the Four Hens.

I went in and put my hand on her shoulder.

"Oh, it's you," she said when she turned around. "I was just looking at these rompers. Aren't they sweet?"

"Really sweet," I said.

"And so tiny," said Helle.

"Big enough," I said. "Are you going to get them?"

"Boys don't wear pink," said Helle.

"We'll take them," I said.

Helle stood in front of me and paid. I had an impulse to kiss her. So without thinking I bent forward and touched her bare shoulder with my dry and chapped lips. What was I playing at? An autumnal breeze blew through my ear, sweeping my thoughts along with it.

The tiny chapel was almost empty. That's how it goes when you lie in bed all day and listen to the radio, I figured. That's what happens when you drink too much red wine and only eat cabbage. If you want your friends to come to your funeral you have to go out into the fresh air and earn them.

The coffin stood on the floor with a single wreath on it and Herman sat on the very front pew, alone. Even if he didn't look like he was grieving, there was a pensive air about him. He was now the oldest living member of the family. It meant that he now had the duty of keeping the family tree in order and putting flowers on all the graves.

We sat in the pew behind Herman. Higgins, Haagen, Hagbart, Helle, Harald and myself. We sat and looked a bit at the coffin whilst the organist limbered up with a bit of light dinner music. Then Haagen got up and played "Öppna landskap" as if he had never played anything else. We all sat there with tears in our eyes, thinking about the fleeting nature of our lives and how important it is to take care of each other.

The vicar talked for a long time about faith and respect.

Then without a hint of trepidation he threw himself into the task of rattling off a long list of details about Mrs Høilund's life. He started with the break-up of the union in 1905, cut through the depression in the thirties, paused for a moment for the war before he landed softly amidst Hulda's final years with her ear close to the transistor radio made by an unknown manufacturer. The high point was an engaging description of fluoroscope photography in 1967. Then it went quiet and the vicar signalled that I should come forward. I walked towards the coffin and stood in front of it. A distant drumming sounded from the second pew where Haagen and Hagbart were playing a sombre accompaniment as a final greeting to Aunt Hulda. I opened my mouth and spoke with loud and clear voice:

Touch on me
Touch me on
I'll be gone
In a couple of days

So unnecessary to comment
I'm jumbled up
But that's me, stumbling along
Slowly realising that life is OK
Repeat what I say
It's no better to be secure than regret

Touch on me
Touch me on
I'll be gone
In a couple of days

The waiting-room was deserted except for the two of us. It was big and white and on the wall there was a poster announcing that the painter Frans Widerberg was to hold an exhibition at some point in the 1980s. It said something along the lines that everyone was welcome, so bring along your mother-in-law and your old lady and come and buy something. A man, hovering over some kind of earthly landscape illustrated the offer.

"I'm going to the toilet," said Helle.

"Go on then," I said.

"Can you look after my bag?" she said.

"Like a guardsman!" I said, grabbing it tightly.

Outside the window the wind whisked around the treetops in the hospital grounds and the rain beat against the window pane. All the songbirds had gone to Spain ages ago.

I lifted Helle's bag up on to my lap. There was no one nearby but you had to be careful. I had bitter experience. I really did.

Helle's mobile phone rang. I looked at the number. It was an internal number at Verdens Gang, the newspaper.

Now that the golf season was over, he probably didn't have anything else to do than call round old employees' wives and chat away. I let the phone carry on ringing and delved deep in the bag looking for a few papers held together by a staple at the corner.

Some men make a big deal of the fact that women have untidy bags. They get all worked up and try to get them to clean up regularly. Personally, I'd learned to appreciate this important side of women. I reached into Helle's bag and took out a prospectus from estate agents Hult & Hansén. The property that was on sale was a terraced house on Havreveien in Manglerud. The price wasn't too bad and it had several bedrooms, a basement living room with accompanying garden, weeds and a compost bin.

The telephone rang again when Helle came back from the toilet.

"Don't answer," I said. "It's only Holm."

"What does he want?" asked Helle.

"No idea," I said.

It soon stopped ringing and we remained seated, looking straight ahead, listening to the sound of the air-conditioning.

"Do you know what a TABARD is?" asked Helle.

"Of course," I said.

"Well?"

"It's a sleeveless jerkin consisting of only front and back pieces with a whole for the head."

"Correct!" said Helle.

"It comes from the Old French TABART," I said.

"You really know a lot, don't you?" said Helle.